Little Ship Under Full Sail

AN ADVENTURE IN HISTORY

Janie Lynn Panagopoulos

To the great Students at Conant Elementary!

J. L. Panagopoulos

11.20.98

R

River Road Publications, Inc.

Spring Lake, Michigan

Library of Congress Cataloging-in-Publication Data

Panagopoulos, Janie Lynn.
    Little Ship Under Full Sail / Janie Lynn Panagopoulos.
        p. cm.
    Summary: When her grandchildren arrive at her home, Grandmother
Kinzie tells Eleanor and Juliette the story of their great-grandmother's capture by the Seneca Indians in 1779.
    ISBN 0-938682-46-6
    1. Lytle, Eleanor—Juvenile fiction.   2. Seneca Indians—Juvenile fic-
tion. [1. Lytle, Eleanor—Fiction.   2. Seneca Indians—Fiction.   3. Indians
of North America—Fiction.   4. Indian captivities—Fiction.]   I. Title.
PZ7.P1885Li 1997
[Fic]—dc21
                                                            97-9604
                                                              CIP
                                                               AC

ISBN: 0-938682-46-6
Printed in the United States of America

Dedicated to my husband Dennis who is always supportive and understanding of my work and to my sons Christopher and Nicholas who constantly put up with their mother's unique way of looking at the world. Thank you for your love.

Contents

Chapter 1
A Journey to the Past

Jeff Davis rides a milk-white horse
And Lincoln rides a mule—
Jeff Davis is a gentleman,
And Lincoln is a fool!

There was a commotion on the crowded train car as two little girls stood and sang their song. Astonished, several of the other passengers glared angrily at the girls and their mother.

"Can you imagine the nerve," whispered one woman to another behind gloved hands. "Why, those Confederates should be feeling grateful to escape the South instead of insulting President Lincoln," whispered another.

Embarrassed by her daughters' behavior, Mrs. Gordon tugged Eleanor and Juliette back into their seats. "Before we boarded this train I warned you both," she quietly admonished. "Now look what you have done. We will be lucky if these Northerners don't throw us off the train before we reach Chicago."

Juliette, the younger of the two, frowned at her

mother. "But Mama, I thought you liked Jeff Davis. Papa likes him. Don't you want Papa and President Davis to win the war against the North?"

An older gentleman who sat nearby lowered his newspaper and looked at Mrs. Gordon as he listened for her answer.

"Hush, now, dear. You shouldn't be disturbing the other passengers." Mrs. Gordon smoothed her daughters' skirts and cuddled them close to her side, ignoring all who stared and listened.

As the steam engine noisily chugged along the tracks, Mrs. Gordon sighed, knowing life would never be the same again. Her husband, an officer in the Confederate army, had sent her and their two young children north to her mother's house in Chicago. This miserable Civil War has made a mess of everything, she thought. Why, there is nothing civil about it. Uprooting a wife from her husband and children from their father. There is just no sense to it. Eleanor Gordon watched out the train window and fought back her tears. At her side her two daughters were lulled by the rocking of the train car on its tracks.

Even though she did not share her husband's sense of loyalty to the southern states which had decided to leave the Union and form their own country, Eleanor Gordon was glad her daughters had the nerve to sing that song. Little Juliette had spunk and energy. Eleanor, only two years older, was more reserved like her father and his family. Wouldn't Mr. Gordon be shocked to think his daughters made such a commotion in a public place, even though it was for the Southern cause? Smiling to herself, Mrs. Gordon wiped tears from her eyes and sat straight and proud. This war wasn't going to hurt her family, no matter what. She would see to that.

As the train swayed Eleanor Gordon thought about her husband, a charming Savannah gentleman. She remembered the surprised look in his eyes when he saw her slide down a banister at their very first meeting in the library at Yale University, where he attended college. She knew such behavior wasn't ladylike, but she had a spark of untamed energy just like the frontier village of Chicago, where she grew up. William Gordon found this spunk fascinating. Now it seemed that together they had passed the spunk, energy, and Southern charm to their daughters, especially Juliette.

"Mama, when can we eat?" Juliette interrupted her mother's daydream. "I'm hungry."

"Me, too," Eleanor added.

Mrs. Gordon sorted through her carpet bag and brought out cloth napkins filled with sweet corn bread, slices of ham from their own smokehouse back home, and apples. She also opened a flask of cider. The three gave thanks and ate their meal.

"Tomorrow, girls," she whispered, "we'll all eat at your Grandmother Kinzie's table."

"How far do we have to go, Mama?" inquired Juliette. "How far to Chicago?"

"It won't be long now. We'll sleep one more night on the train, and we should be there in the morning."

"I don't like sleeping on this train. It hurts my bones," Eleanor complained.

"Well, when we get to Grandmother Kinzie's house you'll forget all about your sore bones. She has feather ticks so big you'll feel like you are floating on a cloud."

The girls' eyes grew wide and they smiled. "I think I'll like it at Grandmother Kinzie's house," said Eleanor.

"Especially if we can sleep in clouds," added

Juliette.

"Did you like living in Chicago, Mama? Will we see Indians?" Juliette thought a moment, then added to her list of questions: "Why don't the people in Chicago like Jeff Davis?"

Mrs. Gordon's face turned red with surprise. "Hush, now," she said, hoping no one had overheard. "Juliette, you certainly ask a lot of questions! Let's get out our blankets and pillows before it's too dark to find our things."

"Will you tell us about Grandma and Grandpa Kinzie and what it was like to grow up in Chicago?" asked Eleanor.

"Yes. Now take your quilts and snuggle down." Mrs. Gordon pulled down quilts and pillows from a shelf above their seat and handed them to Eleanor and Juliette. The girls unlaced their boots and set them neatly beside each other so they could find them in the morning. Wiggling and squirming, they settled into the seat.

"Tomorrow night you can put on your nightgowns and crawl into a real bed," Mrs. Gordon promised.

"And we can fall asleep in a cloud made of feathers," Juliette added. She was tired of the long journey by train and could not wait to get to her grandparents' house.

Once the girls were settled, Mrs. Gordon began describing her family. "We were important people in the town when I grew up," she told them. "Your grandfather first came to Chicago when it was only a swampy wilderness. He was an Indian agent and took care of the business between the Indians of the region and the United States Government."

"Was Grandfather a brave man, Mama?" asked Eleanor.

"Yes, your grandfather was a very brave man and still is. He was the first president of what is now the grand city of Chicago. Of course, it was just a village then. When your grandparents first came, there were only about fifty people. Now there are over one hundred thousand people living there!

"I grew up playing outside through all kinds of weather. We ran through the woods and climbed trees."

"Papa says it is not ladylike to climb trees," Eleanor stated.

"Why, your father knows I used to climb trees and am every bit a lady!"

"You used to slide down banisters in the library at Papa's college. That's what Papa said," giggled Juliette as she imagined her mother sliding down a banister in a wide hoop skirt.

"Yes, and I could still slide down a banister if I had a mind to!" The girls laughed.

"Of course, your grandmother insisted that we be educated. So much of our time in the winter was spent learning how to read and write and cipher. Then when I was older, Grandma sent me off to a girls school in the East where I could learn to be a proper lady. I met your father while I was there, and you know the rest of the story."

"Will we see Indians in Chicago?" asked Juliette who wasn't ready for sleep.

"Probably not, and if we do they will not be like the Indians that once lived there. They are more 'citified' now — more like we are. Your grandmother wrote and told me how she misses seeing her old Potawatomi and Winnebago friends. Sometimes she does see one or two come in from the prairies and just stand on the street corner. They seem amazed that the place is so different now."

"That's sad, Mama," said Juliette.

"Well, I think they would rather live in the wilderness with its fresh air and sunshine than in the modern cities, so smoky from coal dust and noisy with all the people. There is plenty of wilderness out there for them, and there always will be. And most of them are entitled to land on reservations out west."

"What are reservations?" Eleanor asked.

"Areas of land set aside by the U. S. Government just for Indians to live."

"Are they nice places? Can we go to visit Indians there?" Juliette's eyes lit up with this new possibility.

"They are a long way from here, dear, and your grandpa told me once that he thought the Indians were only getting land that no one else wanted. So I don't think it would be a very nice place to visit.

"Of course, there are not as many Indians as there used to be. When I was a girl we used to have dozens of Indian families come to visit. I thought most of them were very nice. Your grandfather had lots of Indian friends. He said they were fine people and gravely misunderstood.

"I remember when I was small there was an epidemic of smallpox that killed many of the

Indians. A lot of them were friends of our family."

"Can't white people get smallpox?" asked Eleanor.

"Well, yes, Eleanor, but it was harder on the Indians. At that time I heard my father say that he feared one day there would be no Indians left at all. They will have just vanished. That makes me sad to think about it. All those people, the friends I once had.... Still, we live in different worlds now. I can't worry about the war and the Indians!"

Mrs. Gordon was now talking to herself. The girls had fallen asleep with the stories and the sway of the train car.

When Mrs. Gordon woke the girls the next morning, they were already in Chicago. Juliette did not think she liked the look of this Chicago. She had hoped for a frontier town, but this was a messy, noisy city. The railroad station was busy and confusing. Callers yelled out the names of places such as Detroit and Kankakee to the crowds waiting for trains.

Amid all the activity Juliette noticed a strongly built, older gentleman staring at them. As her mother turned to scan the crowd, a look of recognition passed over his face along with a broad smile.

He immediately headed in their direction.

"Eleanor! As I live and breathe, daughter, you've made it home. Thank goodness you and the little ones are safe!" The man's strong arms encircled his daughter, and the two hugged as if somehow they could squeeze away the many years they had been separated.

"Is this my grandfather?" Juliette shouted above the noise of the station.

"Why, who do we have here?" asked the old man as he turned his attention to the girls.

Eleanor politely smiled at her grandfather and curtsied.

"Father, these are your granddaughters. This is Eleanor."

John Harrison Kinzie looked into the little girl's face. "Why, look at you! My own daughter's namesake and pretty as a picture. You look just like your mother at that age. And this one?" He turned to Juliette. "This can't be the baby!"

"I'm no baby! I'm Juliette!"

"Why, yes you are. And do you know you are named for your grandmother?"

Juliette studied her grandfather and nodded.

"Girls, give your grandfather a kiss. He has

waited a long time to see you."

Grandfather Kinzie reached down with his strong arms and scooped both of them up. The girls squealed with delight and wrapped their arms around his neck as they kissed him.

"Let's go home, children! I have made arrangements to have your trunks and bags delivered to the house. A carriage awaits my princesses." He motioned toward an area full of wagons and carriages.

The carriage ride through the muddy, narrow streets seemed to Juliette to take forever. This was a city quite different from Savannah, Georgia, where moss hung from beautiful trees. Here were stables, lumberyards, churches, and houses filled with families all crowded together. It looked like a place that had grown so fast that there had been no time to make it beautiful.

As they traveled, Mrs. Gordon chatted with her father, who was pointing out the many changes that had taken place in the city. The girls listened as he showed them the new water works and streets lined with shops where there used to be an apple orchard and an Indian encampment.

"Grandpa, will you show us some Indians if

you see them?" asked Juliette.

"Juliette Gordon, don't be rude! I told you many of the Indians here today look just like you and I."

"I know, Mama, but I would like to see one anyway."

"Well, my darling, I'll tell you what. When we get home I bet your grandmother will be more than happy to share some of her stories with you. I will even lay odds that she will show you some of the gifts that the Indian women gave her many years ago. She has moccasins and baskets and even a cradleboard that your grandfather traveled in when he was just a baby."

Eleanor poked her sister in delight and the girls held hands, hardly able to wait to meet their grandmother.

The old family home was large, and two dogs came barking from behind it as the carriage pulled up in front. The door of the frame house opened and there stood a smart-looking, gray-haired woman in a pink floral dress. "Girls, there's your grandmother," Mrs. Gordon announced lovingly.

The family jumped from the carriage and soon found themselves in the warmth of the Kinzie home. "How was your trip, darling? Is this little Eleanor? Have you heard from William? He was a smart man to send you all to us. This can't be Juliette! She was just a baby —"

"Now, dear, let them settle in and rest before you exhaust them with questions. They've had a long journey," said Grandfather Kinzie.

"I know, but there is just so much to catch up on," said the older woman. "My daughter is home, safe and sound with her own little angels." Mrs. Kinzie dabbed the end of her nose with her handkerchief as tears rolled down her cheeks. "As soon as your trunks and bags arrive from the station you should all go upstairs and freshen up. Your father is right. You have had a long journey."

"Oh, Mother, we are so glad to be here! The trip was horrid and the people on the train car were so uncivil."

"Grandma, will you tell us about the Indians?" asked Juliette.

"Oh, my! What is this?" replied Grandmother Kinzie in surprise.

"Juliette," Mrs. Gordon scolded, "mind your manners."

"Oh, no, Eleanor, don't scold her."

Grandmother Kinzie stooped down beside Juliette and cuddled her in her arms. "You know, I have some wonderful stories about Indians. They are a mighty fine people, and many are my friends. But we'll have plenty of time for stories after you and your mama and sister have had a chance to get something to eat. How does that sound?"

Juliette smiled and nodded.

"Oh, Mother, don't go and spoil these girls while we are here. You know how important it is that they mind their manners."

"Yes, dear, you are absolutely right. Just like I never spoiled any of you children."

"I seem to remember a little girl who liked to sass her mother and climb trees and hide when it was time to do her chores," Grandfather Kinzie added.

"Now, Father, please. The girls do not need to hear any stories about my childhood. Mother always said I was the perfect child, didn't you, Mother?"

"I think your mother always said you were a perfect rascal!"

Little Eleanor and Juliette giggled at their grandfather's comment.

"Oh, Father! How could you say that in front of the children. Do you know how hard it is to raise these two all by myself since William has been off to war?"

"Yes, dear, you have been through a lot. But now we can help."

"Grandmother Kinzie, did you carry your babies on your back like an Indian lady?"

"Juliette!"

"It's all right, daughter. She is only curious, just like you when you were young. In fact, I'd say from what you've written me and what I've heard so far, that Juliette is another Little Ship Under Full Sail."

"Mother, I haven't heard that name in years."

"Well, I don't suppose you have, living the life of a fine lady of the South."

"Oh, Mother . . .."

"What is Little Ship Under Full Sail?" interrupted Eleanor.

"Oh, my darling, that's a very special name."

"What does it mean?"

"Well, it was a name once given to your great-grandmother, Eleanor Lytle Kinzie because she was such a strong-hearted girl and not afraid to speak her mind — just like your mama."

"Great-grandmother's name was Eleanor, too, just like Mama's and mine?"

"Yes, just like yours and your mama's. But she had another name given her by the Indians. That was Little Ship Under Full Sail. Did you know your great-grandmother was once a captive of the Indians?"

The girls stood wide-eyed. "A captive? You mean, she was a prisoner?"

"That's the story I'm going to tell you after you've freshened up and we have had some dinner," Grandmother Kinzie promised.

It seemed to Eleanor and Juliette that settling in at the Kinzie's took much longer than necessary. But finally they were curled up with their grandmother on the sofa in the parlor, ready for the story.

"The year," Grandmother Kinzie began, "was 1779, another time when our nation was at war. We were just thirteen states then and had declared ourselves a new nation. But first we had to fight with Great Britain, which did not want to give us our independence. Your great-grandmother, whose name was Eleanor Lytle (but everyone called her

Nellie), was living in the wilderness of western
Pennsylvania with her family. . .."

Chapter 2
Capture!

Nellie could feel the first hints of autumn coolness in the late summer afternoon. It was a beautiful day. The sky was a deep cloudless blue and a few patches of leaves already yellow and red could be seen in the great forest that surrounded their cabin. Nellie and her brother Robert had finished their chores, and it was naptime for their younger siblings.

Nellie loved this time of day. Mama wanted Robert and her out of the house so the little ones could nap in peace. She seemed to enjoy using this quiet time to attend to her wheel, combing and spinning the wool from their sheep so that she could make winter clothes for the family. Papa was usually gone from the cabin in the afternoon. He worked in the fields, hunted, or like today, helped one of their distant neighbors build a barn.

Nellie and Robert played in the field beside the cabin. They liked to imagine they were officers in the American army, leading their troops against the British. Like their parents, Nellie and Robert never tired of hearing news of the war that had

now been going on for three years. The children
felt certain the Americans would win their fight
against the British and be a free nation. But their
parents warned that this might not happen. The
British had well-trained soldiers and the money to
buy weapons and other supplies. They also had
many Indians on their side, including some of the
powerful Iroquois tribes. The Americans, on the
other hand, had little or no training and few supplies. It was as if the American army was a young
boy pitted against a mighty giant — the British
army.

"Do you hear that?" Robert stopped his play
and listened. "There it is again. First there's the
sound of a bird call, and then there's another call,
like an answer." The two children stood quietly and
listened. "Sometimes Indians give signals like that,
and I think I saw one this morning when I was out
chopping wood. He was out just past the meadow."

Knowing her younger brother's imagination
often played tricks on him, Nellie started to shake
her head. But at that instant a figure passed
through the shadows of the distant trees. Startled,
the two ran for the cabin.

"Ma! Come and look!" Robert burst through the

door first, waking their little brother and sister.

"Someone's in the woods beyond the clearing. I think I saw something out there. And I heard something," said Robert.

"Mama, there really was," added Nellie. "Maybe you should get the gun."

"It could be an Indian," added Robert, who was seven and very intrigued by Indians.

Their mother looked up from her spinning and shook her head at her older children's fright and the wide eyes of the younger ones who were now climbing down from the bed. "Did you two ever take into account that it might be the cow? Or what about a deer? I saw a doe and her fawn out on the edge of the meadow myself just this morning. Besides, we know the names and clan of every Indian within ten miles of here, and they're all our friends.

"You know, Robert, you are a skittish boy, and the two of you are always causing unnecessary alarm. I think those settlers' children down the way have frightened you to death with all their stories about war and scalping. I will tell your pa I don't want you two to go visiting them if you can't keep your wits about you. Do you understand?

"Now go back to your play—and learn to be of more courage. What is a man without courage, Robert?"

Robert hung his head as Nellie looked crossly at him. This was the second time in a week he had gotten her into trouble.

"That's it, you two. Now scat. How can I get these little ones to nap and do my spinning with you running around all wild-like? Go outside and play."

Bounding out the cabin door, the two children soon forgot their scolding. Nellie ran to the well and lowered the bucket into the cool black pool below. Robert joined her and together they cranked the handle, bringing up the bucket filled with cold water. Nellie took the dipper from its nail and both drank greedily.

Dropping the bucket back into the well, Nellie slapped Robert on the back. "You're IT," she yelled as she ran around the side of the cabin. "And don't forget to hang up the dipper."

"No fair, Nellie Lytle," Robert yelled back as he fumbled with the dipper. "I didn't know we were playing tag!" He stretched to find the nail, being careful not to drop the dipper into the well. He had

done that recently and made his mother plenty
mad at him. Then he darted off to find his sister.

Nellie ran beyond the cabin and past the out-
house and the small barn that their father had
built with the help of other settlers in the area.
The long grass, now dry and turning yellow, whispered around her long skirts.

Robert called from behind her and followed her
path through the sunny field toward the edge of
the forest. His legs pushed through the tall grass
and butterflies tumbled before him. Along the forest edge he could see where his father had girdled
trees in preparation for a larger barn to be built
next spring.

Just then Robert saw a flash of movement. It
was the doe and fawn that his mother had seen
earlier. He breathed a sigh of relief. His mother
was right, as always; the figure he had spotted in
the shadows must have been the deer.

In the peace of the afternoon Nellie soon forgot
about the game of tag she had started. She slowed
to a walk in the tall grass, listening to the chatter
of the insects. Her brother caught up with her, but
happily abandoned the game of tag he knew he
couldn't win.

"I think bugs talk to each other," Nellie explained to her brother.

"Little Bear says the bugs and trees and animals and rocks all talk." Robert was pleased to be able to tell his sister what his Indian friend had told him. "He says we just have to learn to listen. He says we've got to have respect for them and live peacefully with them."

Nellie thought for a moment. "Well, we are not living very peacefully with the trees when we cut them down. And Little Bear is not living very peacefully with animals when he shoots a squirrel."

Robert scrunched his face. "I think we can use stuff, like trees for our barn, or shoot animals for food. But we shouldn't just do it for no reason – just waste it. I think that's what Little Bear meant."

Robert was proud of having an Indian friend, and he thought about all he had learned from him. Suddenly he felt as if this knowledge gave him new power over his older sister. "Little Bear says his people give names that have meaning. Like the Ohio River. Oh-he-ho, he says, means 'beautiful.'

"I would like to be an Indian, an Iroquois. I

heard Pa say that even Ben Franklin in Philadelphia believes the Iroquois are very smart people. He studied their government to help make our own government. Pa says the Iroquois run their nation better than old Mother England ever ran this one. And the Indians stick together. They are not like us Americans, Tories fighting against their own Patriot neighbors because they think we should stick with old England!"

"That's not true, Robert. You don't know half what you think you do! Pa said the Iroquois nation is all broken up over this war. Some chiefs like the British, and some like us Americans, like Little Bear's clan. Some still like the Frenchies best of all, even though the British chased them out years ago."

"The Frenchies don't like to wash, you know," Robert burst out with some new information. "Mama said she met a French trader once that had never taken a full wash in his whole life, and he smelled like it. But he picked his teeth with hazel bush sticks, like the Indians, and he had the prettiest white teeth she had ever seen."

"Maybe his face was so dirty it just made his teeth look white," Nellie suggested.

Robert giggled and slapped his sister on the back with new enthusiasm. "You're IT!" he yelled and ran toward the woods.

Nellie raced after her brother, her bare feet stinging from the dry grass. Her brother was now out of sight in the piles of brush that had been trimmed from the logs used to build their barn and left along the edge of the forest. Suddenly he popped up from behind a pile to scare his sister. "Robert!" she scolded after recovering from her fright.

Deciding it was time for a new game, Nellie headed for a large fallen tree. She hoisted her skirt and climbed on, straddling it as if it were a horse. "Come on, Robert, ride to battle with me. I'm General George Washington!"

Robert mounted the tree-horse behind his sister and grabbed a stick in his hand. "Come to battle, you blasted Red Coats. I dare you to tell me what taxes I have to pay!"

"Robert! Did you hear that?" Nellie's voice was suddenly serious. "I think I hear the bird calls again."

"They must be real birds, not Indian signals. Mama says all the Indians around here are our friends and that — ."

Nellie put out her hand to quiet her brother. They both heard the call of a quail from the nearby woods. It was followed by the hoot of an owl.

Nellie dismounted the tree-horse and stared into the woods, filled with fear.

"Nellie!" screamed Robert.

A hand from behind her quickly slid over Nellie's mouth. She felt another hand grab her by the hair and jerk her head back so far all she could see was the sky. The hand then released her hair and a strong arm seized her around the waist. At the same moment she saw an Indian whose face was covered with paint pull Robert off the tree. These were not their friends, the Indians from their valley. . ..

Nellie struggled, but a large man with an iron grip held her firmly. Meanwhile the man who had grabbed Robert pushed him to the ground. When Nellie reached out to help him, her captor yanked her away. Don't fight, she told herself, as she remembered terrifying stories of those who had struggled with Indian enemies.

As their captors dragged them into the dark shadows of the woods Nellie saw several other

Indians, all unfamiliar to her, crawling through the meadow toward the cabin. Seconds later she heard the screams of her mother and the cries of her little brother and sister.

"Mama," sobbed Robert as he struggled helplessly in the grasp of the strong warrior.

Nellie felt her heart in her throat as she watched smoke rise from the cabin roof.

Quickly the Indians connected Nellie and Robert with long leather cords, one binding their wrists, and another with nooses around their necks. Two men, one in front and one behind, held the cords, pulling the children deeper into the woods and away from the sight of the burning cabin.

On a forest trail the Indians broke into a run, with their young captives stumbling along. Nellie remembered stories from their neighbors about captives who were killed because they couldn't keep up. Just then Robert stumbled and fell face forward on the forest floor, landing with a grunt and thump. His fall jerked Nellie backward, the leather tie cutting into her neck. In their rush the Indians pulled Robert along on his knees as he struggled to get up.

"Stop! Stop! He's hurt," Nellie yelled at the men.

Surprised by her outburst, the Indians paused for a moment and pulled Robert to his feet. The man in front pulled the rope, but Nellie resisted. "Are you all right, Robert?"

Robert nodded, but Nellie saw blood begin to trickle from a cut on his forehead and knew he was about to cry. "It will be all right," she promised. "Just try to keep up and don't cry."

Robert nodded again. Nellie knew he remembered the stories, too.

Chapter 3

Prisoners

The warriors led their captives into the green
shade of the woods to a creek where Nellie and
Robert sometimes played. Plunging into the ankle-
deep water, the four waded down the stream so
that the two Indians could be sure they would not
leave an escape trail.

Nellie, who was barefoot, stumbled along on
the jagged rocks. She winced at every stab on her
tender feet until at last they throbbed with such
pain that the new jabs and insults could hardly be
felt. The threats of what might happen to her
loomed larger than her pain, and she concentrated
on keeping her footing.

The Indians who had captured them were tall
and strong and painted with black and red paint
made from ashes and minerals. Nellie knew these
were colors of war and death. It was clear that she
and Robert were now in the hands of enemies.

Robert let out a cry as he was jerked along by
the leather rope.

"Hush, brother. Be brave. Remember the stories," Nellie warned. She turned to see if her

brother had heard her and saw the fear in his eyes. He's only seven, she thought to herself. I must be the brave one.

Although Nellie was terrified, she began to think more clearly about their situation. She knew the Indians appreciated courage and bravery, so she should not allow them to see her fear. She hoped Robert also would try to be strong.

After a time the four left the creek and turned up a steep hill along a worn deer path. The leather bindings jerking at her wrists, Nellie ran along behind the warrior to the top of the hill where they plunged down a wooded gully. Limbs and branches lashed at their faces as they went headlong into the undergrowth.

The first warrior, continually trying to keep up the group's speed through the tangled woods, hopped over a large fallen limb that lay across their path. As Nellie tried to do the same, her foot caught in the hem of her long skirt, and she fell headfirst to the ground. The leather thongs that held her wrists cut deep into her skin, while the noose around her neck jerked Robert off his feet and on top of her.

Hurt and bleeding, Nellie fought back the

tears. But Robert, who had the wind knocked out of him, started to cry. Nellie quickly reached to put her hand to his mouth and quiet him. Just then the lead man, who had been yanked backwards by the weight of the fall, pulled sharply on Nellie's thongs, trying to drag her to her feet and untangle the children. With all her strength Nellie yanked back, jerking the man's arms.

"He's hurt, can't you see?" shouted Nellie. The Indian lunged at Nellie but hesitated when he saw her fierce stare.

The second man laughed, making fun of his companion for fighting with a child. Then he untangled Robert and helped him to his feet. Next he reached for Nellie, who refused his hand. Stubbornly she pulled herself onto her elbows and knees and then managed to get her stubbed and bleeding feet under her. How she wished she had listened to Mama's advice about wearing her boots when she played.

As the group resumed their travel, the lead man moved them more slowly through the thick woods. After a short time they came to a ridge that looked down over a valley. There a ribbon of gray smoke curled up from the chimney of a small cabin. Nellie guessed that this was the cabin of an old hermit she had heard her father speak about. The man had lived in the area longer than any other settler and rarely spoke to anyone. Nellie doubted that he would be the type to rescue them.

It's no use, she said to herself. She could think of no one who could save them, unless their father had somehow come home early. And what had happened to Mama and the babies? She shuddered as she remembered their screams and cries.

Nellie was too afraid to think about this now. She had to make sure that Robert kept up and that he didn't cause their captors any trouble. Meanwhile, her feet were numb and her legs throbbed with pain. Show them you are brave, she told herself. There were stories about children who were captured by the enemy and then caused trouble. She knew there were crosses in cemeteries for some of these children.

As they followed the ridge Nellie wondered how much farther they would travel. She had never been this far, and the forest seemed endless. She looked back along their path. If she and Robert had a chance to escape, they would have to return this way. It seemed impossible, but she must try to remember every creek, gully, ridge, and meadow.

Just then Nellie heard a low rumbling sound. Although there were now some clouds in the sky, it did not look or feel like rain. Still, Nellie thought, it must be thunder. As they traveled the land sloped downward. The forest floor, which had been soft, was now rocky. The sound that resembled thunder became a rolling, bubbling roar. It was a large river, a place that Nellie had heard about, a dangerous place.

From stories, Nellie knew that when settlers first came to the valley they took rafts down a great river to the rapids. But before they reached this place they put ashore because the rapids were too long and too rough. Some who tried to go farther capsized and lost all their belongings. Some lost their lives. Nellie had heard her father say that the river brought people to the valley and the rapids kept them there.

Suddenly the two men stopped. The leader dropped the leather ropes and disappeared down along the water's edge. The other sat down on a rock and motioned the children to sit.

Nellie turned to Robert. Dust and tears streaked his face and his nose was runny. She noticed dried blood at the corners of his mouth. When she was sure they weren't being watched, she smiled cautiously, hoping to make her brother feel better. But he just looked away, wiping his nose on his shirt sleeve.

The Indian pulled out a water bladder from a pouch at his side and gave the children a drink. Then he took a knife and began cutting pieces off a chunk of dried meat and eating them. Robert reached out with his tied wrists toward the man, who quickly jerked the blade of his knife back. Frightened, Robert also pulled back.

"I think he thought you were trying to take his knife. Put your tongue out so he can put the meat in your mouth," Nellie instructed.

Robert lifted his face and opened his mouth wide, sticking out his tongue. The man leaned forward and placed a slice of meat in his mouth. Robert grabbed the meat and ripped off a piece for Nellie. It was tough and hard to chew, but both children were so hungry that even the toughest meat tasted good. Robert smiled up at the man, who now cut more slices for them.

Just then the other Indian dashed up to the rocky ledge and spoke hurriedly to his partner,

pointing along the ridge. Grabbing the leather
lines, the man yanked Nellie and Robert to their
feet as the second Indian put the food into his
pouch. Then they started down to the river's edge.

The trail to the river was well-marked with
slashes and dabs of Indian paint and travel was
easier. As they walked Nellie watched the river
spill white foam over ledges, rocks, and boulders as
it forced its way downstream.

"We can't cross here, Nellie. I can't swim. We
can't cross here," cried a panicked Robert.

Nellie agreed silently as the four made their
way along the edge of the angry water. Suddenly
she was nearly overcome by the smells around her
— the damp smell of wet limestone, the stinking
rot of dead plants and fish, and the odor of her own
battered and sweating body. She had never felt like
this before — exhausted, frightened, and broken.
She prayed the Indians would stop as she picked
up one bruised foot after the other, following the
lead of her captor.

The day wore on. It seemed to Nellie that they
had followed the river trail for hours. She was now
in great pain and very hungry. Occasionally she
managed to glance around at Robert. He seemed to

be in a daze as he followed her. He no longer cried,
and tears no longer stained his cheeks. He just
followed.

The long rapids that had frightened the children gave way to quieter waters with some wide
open areas. Nellie hoped the Indians had hidden
canoes somewhere along the river's banks so that
she would no longer have to walk.

Twilight began to cast its long, rose-colored
shadows along the treeline. The two warriors
stopped, each pointing to different places along the
opposite side of the river. Finally, the first man
plunged into the water and planted his feet in the
current, pulling Nellie in after him with the
leather cord.

For a moment the water seemed cold and
painful, but soon Nellie was thankful for the relief
it brought to her swollen, bloody feet. Moving
ahead one step at a time, she braced herself
against the current. Robert followed, holding his
bound wrists above his head for balance.

The farther into the river the group went, the
harder it was for them to keep their feet on the
river bottom. Suddenly, Nellie's feet slipped on a
moss-covered rock and she was swept into the

current. Yanked by the leather line, Robert was
also pulled beneath the water. For a moment the
Indian behind Robert struggled to hold his own
footing. Then he pulled Robert's neck noose tight
and brought the boy's head above water.

Meanwhile Nellie managed to get her head
above water and regain her footing. The Indian in
the lead held tight to the line as if to keep her from
being swept away again. The second Indian lifted
Robert from the water and threw the boy on his
shoulder. He then dragged Nellie at his side as he
made his way to the opposite shore.

Exhausted and trembling, Robert and Nellie
climbed up the bank with the help of their captors.
Nellie's long skirts, now soaking wet, clung to her
legs and pulled at her waist and hips.

"Please, please!" she cried to the men who were
already tugging at the lines to move the children
on once again. "Please wait!"

The men stopped. With her bound hands Nellie
began twisting the water out of her heavy wet
skirts, wishing she were wearing pants like Robert.
That gave her an idea. She pulled the back hem of
her skirt forward between her legs and tucked the
wet material up into the front waistband. Now the

skirt was an awkward type of pants. This will help, she thought.

The small band proceeded silently and slowly, the children exhausted. The dark trail along the river eventually led them to a clearing where they could see the early stars starting to shine. Nellie prayed they would stop. Robert stumbled along the trail, walking with his eyes shut and his head bobbing back and forth as if he were asleep on his feet.

Suddenly the Indians picked up their pace, yanking both captives forward. They seemed to recognize the area and talked quietly to each other in hurried tones. Then they stopped, dropping the children's ropes. The lead Indian disappeared into the forest while the second stood watch over the captives. He pointed to the ground, and Robert collapsed onto his knees, pulling Nellie with him. Cold and still wet from the river, the children huddled together and shared each other's warmth.

After several minutes Nellie heard the quiet voices of men approaching. The Indian guarding them listened closely. Soon several men came out of the shadows. They greeted the guard and looked down at the children.

Just then the lead Indian rejoined the group.

He pulled a long sharp knife from his woven belt and bent over Nellie. Startled, she pulled back. But the Indian just laughed and reached for her tightly bound wrists. As he cut through her leather thongs Nellie's arms fell limp. Then she rubbed the swollen, bruised wrists and felt the blood pulse back into her numb hands.

Robert, who had nearly fallen asleep, quickly sat up and offered his tied wrists to the Indian with the knife. The men laughed at the boy's lack of fear. Nellie noticed that both their captors seemed to have grown cheerful in the company of their friends. It reminded her of Papa when his friends stopped by to pay a visit.

After pulling the children to their feet two of the men scooped up Nellie and Robert and flung them over their shoulders. Then the group began to travel again. This time it was a short trip. They had not gone far when the man carrying Nellie lowered her to the ground. The other man also dropped Robert, who moved close to his sister.

"Nellie, I'm cold," whined Robert. Nellie reached out and drew her little brother closer. She was cold, too, but she doubted that the Indians would build a fire tonight and expose their hiding place.

Just then several of the men brought out calico bed sheets that Nellie thought had probably come from some settlers' cabin. They spread them on the ground and then set out some smoked ham and corn bread.

"Nellie, I'm thirsty," Robert complained again. It had been hours since they had water and Nellie understood his need. Putting her hands together to make the shape of a cup, she brought it to her lips as if to drink.

One of the Indians pulled out a small keg and removed a cork. "I think it's liquor, Robert. Don't drink it," Nellie whispered to her brother. The Indian offered the keg to the children, but Nellie shook her head and pushed it away.

The men laughed. The one who had given them a bladder of water before offered it to them again. Robert grabbed it and drank eagerly, the water drizzling down his chin. Wiping his face, he gave it to Nellie who finished off the contents. The water was warm and stale, but it was wet and quenched their thirst.

After they drank the water the Indians motioned for them to eat. Desperately hungry, both stuffed their mouths with the ham and corn bread. But Nellie lost her appetite when she realized that these Indians did not meet accidentally. This was not Indian food. They had been raiding settler's cabins. This was part of a plan.

Were there other captives? Nellie shivered with fear. A deep sadness overtook her once again as she thought about her mother and her little brother and sister.

The men now wrapped themselves in blankets, another item Nellie feared may have come from settlers' cabins. But when they handed blankets to her and Robert, her fear gave into relief. At least the Indians were sharing with them.

Cuddled together, the exhausted children started to drift off to sleep. In the distance Nellie heard a wolf howling, calling for its mate. Nellie wondered if it felt as lonesome in the wilderness that night as she did. She wished for a small warm fire to brighten the dark night.

They had not been sleeping long when a sound in the forest brought everyone to attention. Nellie sat up straight and quickly shook Robert from his sleep. She wondered if it was the wolf she had heard earlier. Nellie had been told that if she was

ever caught in the wilderness overnight she should
start a fire to keep the wolves and other wild animals away. But in the moon's reflection there was
no safety except for the protection of her captors.

But where were her captors? Nellie tried to
make out the outlines of the men in the night, but
it was almost impossible to see anything. Finally,
in the distance she made out some shapeless forms
of people walking and huddling together. Maybe it
was Pa coming to rescue them. Her heart raced.
Robert clung to her and buried his head in her
shoulder.

Soon the frightened children heard the call of a
quail. They recognized it as the same call they had
heard while playing near the cabin before their
capture. It was answered by the call of an owl.
Nellie now knew that it wasn't her father. Afraid of
what was happening, Nellie and Robert held tight
to each other and pulled their blankets over their
heads.

No sooner had they hidden themselves when a
hand grabbed hold of Nellie's hair right through
the blanket. Stifling a cry, she put her hands over
her mouth and rose painfully to her stiff feet.
Robert, also aching and sore from the day's adven-

tures, struggled to his feet and stood beside her,
holding his blanket tightly.

The hand that pulled Nellie's hair now let it
fall. The children stood in the darkness as a great
shadow loomed over them. Then other figures
moved into the camp, picking up the children and
throwing them over their shoulders. Running like
deer they carried the small captives into the black-
ness of night.

Neither the frightened Nellie or Robert cried
out. Instead they endured the jostling until the
men stopped and flipped them onto the ground.
Nellie had squeezed her eyes so tightly shut that
she had trouble opening them.

Ever so slowly she opened her eyes to a squint
and saw a small fire. Robert lay motionless beside
her, his head still covered by his blanket. His still-
ness frightened Nellie, but as she pulled the blanket from his head he sat up and faced the light of
the fire.

In the dim firelight the children could see the
faces of settlers. There were nearly a dozen of them
— captives like themselves. Looking around
quickly Nellie saw one she recognized.

"Mama, Mama," Nellie rose stiffly and started

toward her mother. Just then a big arm reached out and pulled her back sharply. Robert, who had started to follow her, stood silent and still in his tracks. The Indian brought his hand to his mouth and gave a warning of silence.

We are still close enough to a settlement or a search party to be heard, Nellie thought hopefully.

Nellie nodded to the man who released her, and on her sore feet hobbled to her mother's arms. Robert followed and dropped into his mother's lap. He buried his head and silently wept, his body shaking with sobs.

For a moment Nellie and Robert were soothed by their mother's touch. They felt certain their mother would know what to do. She would know if Pa was coming to help them.

But their mother was oddly silent, and in her eyes was a look of terror. She did not, she could not speak of her sadness. Holding her children close, she swayed back and forth in the dim light.

The large Indian that had silenced Nellie came near and placed warm blankets over the small, frightened family. Nellie looked up at the man. She thought she saw a look of kindness in his face, even though he was their enemy.

Chapter 4
Wilderness Rendezvous

The next morning Nellie awoke safe in her mother's arms. Robert lay asleep on the ground beside them.

Nellie watched and listened as the other captives began to stir and speak in hushed, frightened tones. In the distance she could see several Indians gathered who seemed to be deciding what to do. Some spoke in a quiet manner while others paced back and forth wildly, moving their arms in anger.

Nellie decided that the Indians were debating about the captives. Perhaps there were now too many of them to move in a single group. There were other children, too; they would slow the group down.

Nellie's mother stirred. She looked tired, and her hair, which was always braided neatly into a bun, now hung loose and wild. This was not the mother Nellie knew. This was someone as fearful as Nellie herself.

"Mama, Mama," whispered Nellie. Her mother's eyes flew open with a start. "Mama, it's only me. Don't be afraid." Nellie's mother wrapped her arms around her daughter and began to weep.

"Mama, where are the little ones? Where are Tommy and Meggie? Did they get away?"

There was a long pause with no answer. Nellie couldn't understand why her mother wouldn't speak. She just stared into the wilderness with tears rolling down her cheeks.

Nellie studied her mother. She wasn't herself. It was as if something terrible had changed her forever. "I don't know, Nellie," she finally answered, shaking her head and wiping tears on the back of her hand. "I just don't know."

Nellie tried to comfort her mother, but she couldn't speak. She couldn't even swallow. Her throat was dry and tight with emotion. Nellie's nose began to run before she actually felt the burning tears in her eyes. Oh, poor Meggie and Tommy, she thought.

"Mama, when will Papa come with help to find us? As soon as he finds out what has happened he will come, won't he?"

Nellie's mother hung her head and shook it back and forth slowly. "He shouldn't follow. It's too dangerous. It's too dangerous. He has to find the babies. He has to find Tommy and Meggie."

All around her Nellie could now hear soft sighs
of weeping women and children. She recognized a
few of them from church meetings or cabin rais-
ings. Some of the captives were injured, and others
were crying out of despair and fear.

Nellie tried to pull away from her mother, who
still held her oldest child close and rocked her like
a baby. "Mama, please, I have to go make water."

Slowly Mrs. Lytle stopped rocking and released
her grip. "Nellie, before you leave me, listen to
what I have to say. Don't ever forget my words. I
might not have a chance to talk to you again, at
least not for a long while."

Nellie pulled away from her mother. "What are
you saying? Papa will be here soon and rescue us
all. We will all be home with Tommy and Meggie
and Papa soon."

"Hush, child. Look into my eyes and remember
my words."

Nellie sat still and frightened in her mother's
lap, staring into her wild eyes.

"Nellie, you have to be brave. Don't cause a
stir. Just go along with these men. They are not
like our friends from the Indian villages. They are
men at war, and we are their prize."

"What do you mean, prize? What do they want with us?"

"It's likely they want to ransom us for money, food, and guns. It will take time for your father to find us. And he shouldn't follow us right now. That might be the end of us all. He will have to go to Fort Pitt or Fort Niagara for help. That will take time. We have to remain strong and stay together, if we can, until the time comes when he can rescue us.

"You have to remain brave. You are nine years old now. You are strong and smart. You must use your brain. I don't know what will happen now. I am worried about Robert. He is still a child, and his strength might give out. If that happens, I'm afraid to think of what they might do. . .."

"How long will it take Papa to come ransom us?" Nellie interrupted her mother's thoughts.

"I don't know. There are many of us. It may take time for the families to agree on what should be done.

"There are too many of us to travel together," Mrs. Lytle continued. "We three must stay together if possible. It will make it easier for your father to find us. But if we do have to separate, Nellie, let

your brother stay by my side. I will carry him if I
must. You must use all your strength to survive
yourself."

Nellie's heart sank. What was her mother saying? They couldn't be separated. They just couldn't.

"Nellie, do you hear me? If we have to separate, do all you can to make sure Robert comes
with me."

"But Mama —" Nellie's heart broke at the
thought that she might be all alone, without Mama
or Robert. "Mother, I can watch over Robert and
you, too," she pleaded. "I can carry him if I must."

"No. You heard what I said. This is the best
way for us all to survive. You will be able to walk
and do what they ask. Robert will not. You must
live, girl, survive.

"Nellie, my sweet, listen to me. I have already
had a full life. You have to fight for your right to
grow up and have a husband and family, too, and
much more. Robert and I will only hold you back,
and together we might all be destroyed. I will tend
to him. You tend to you. Do you understand, my
love?"

Nellie buried her head deep into her mother's
shoulder. She shook with waves of tears. We have

to stay together, she thought, we just have to.

It was at that moment a hand touched Nellie's shoulder. She could feel her mother's body stiffen with fear. Nellie looked up with her tear-stained face. It was the tall Indian from the night before, the one who made a sign for her to be silent. In his hands he held a clean linen cloth and a pair of moccasins.

Nellie, not wanting to leave her mother's arms, turned away.

"Nellie," her mother said sharply. "Don't insult the man. You know the danger."

Nellie turned back and nodded her thanks. Then she reached out and took the leather slippers. In her heart she was grateful that the man had noticed her bare feet the night before, but to accept kindness from an enemy was a hard thing to do. Slowly sliding off her mother's lap Nellie lifted her skirts, exposing her battered, swollen feet.

"Nellie, you have no boots," her mother cried out. "Oh, Nellie." Mrs. Lytle held back tears when she saw the condition of her daughter's feet. She had thought Nellie would be able to survive by herself, and now she could see that the girl might become a problem to the Indians.

"Can you stand, girl?"

Nellie slowly stood, but her feet stung and throbbed as she put her weight on them. "I can stand. I can walk," she said bravely as she started forward with a painful limp.

"She needs to soak her feet!" Mrs. Lytle cried frantically as she pulled herself to her feet. "She needs medicine. She can walk miles if she has a poultice and salve. I need to get some St. John's Wort and Comfrey."

Startled by the outburst, the tall Indian pushed Nellie's mother back. "Sit," he insisted. His paint-streaked face was strong and powerful, his dark eyes deep and piercing.

"Sit, Mama, sit," Nellie instructed as the big man disappeared through some underbrush.

"For almighty goodness, woman, sit down," called one of the other captives. "You will bring trouble upon all our heads."

Defeated, Mrs. Lytle sat down.

"It's all right, Mama, it's all right," soothed Nellie as she also sat down to put on the moccasins. She knew the moccasins would help. They had to.

Robert, awakened by the commotion, began to

cry. Nellie could see that even though her brother was seven, he was still very much a child and needed the attention of his mother.

"Mama," he whined, "I have to make water." Mrs. Lytle helped him to his feet and pointed to a tree nearby. She dared not move herself without her captor's permission.

"I'll take him, Mama," said Nellie, remembering her own needs. Setting forth carefully on her sore feet, she took her brother's hand. She had to walk to show her mother that no matter how painful it was, she would make it.

After Robert had finished Nellie sent him back to their mother. It was her turn. She was now glad to have long skirts to protect her privacy as she squatted.

Soon she returned to the group. There waiting, was the tall Indian. He had an older man with him who carried a pot of steaming water.

"Sit," he pointed to Nellie and then to the ground. "Sit."

Nellie sat and the Indian pointed to her feet. The older man examined them with an air of authority. His long hair was streaked with gray and woven into a braid. His body gleamed—probably from bear grease, Nellie thought. He knelt over her feet, shook his head, and muttered to the younger man. The younger man's voice rose in disagreement, and he pointed to the steaming pot.

"Put feet here," he said in broken English.

The water steamed in front of Nellie. She knew it had to be very hot. Still, she reasoned, it probably wasn't any hotter than the bath water her mother occasionally made for them. Carefully Nellie lifted her feet and eased them into the water. It felt slimy and held a variety of mashed and boiled plants. The bitter smell of medicine rose from the pot and the hot mixture bit at her cuts, making her feet feel as if they would explode.

"Have courage, daughter, be brave," said her mother as she watched Nellie's face. Robert crawled into his mother's lap and began crying.

"I'm fine, Robert. It's like the bath water Mama makes for us."

"I know," Robert called out. "It must be boiling!"

Nellie's heart lifted a bit as she saw a slight smile creep across her mother's face.

The two Indian men who stood watch soon began a conversation, leaving Nellie to soak her feet. Shortly, the pain and heat began to subside and Nellie felt the concoction begin to soothe away the pain of yesterday. It was magic!

Nellie watched as the Indians spoke. After a time the older man gave the younger one a small leather pouch and walked away.

With the pouch in hand, the younger man approached the little family. With a forceful voice he gave orders to the other Indians who stood nearby. They left and then quickly reappeared with food and bladders of water for the prisoners. He must be some sort of chief or leader, thought Nellie.

Still holding the small pouch, the man sat beside Nellie and her family as they ate. For a few moments it was if they were all just having a picnic in the forest. When they had finished, he directed Nellie to take her feet out of the water, which had now cooled.

Nellie followed his directions and dried her feet with the linen cloth. Carefully, the Indian opened the leather pouch. Inside was another piece of leather and inside that a large leaf folded and pinned with two small twigs. The Indian pulled out the twigs and unfolded the leaf. There was a pink salve with a sweet smell. "It's St. John's Wort," Mrs. Lytle said as she sniffed it.

The Indian handed the salve to Mrs. Lytle and directed her to apply it to Nellie's feet. "The color looks right," she said confidently as she carefully spread the salve. When she had finished she wrapped each foot with cloth she tore from one of her underskirts and tied each piece tightly around Nellie's ankles. The Indian handed Nellie the moccasins, which she slipped over the bandages.

Nellie looked around and wondered at the attention that was given her. Other people were hurt and bruised. Why had the Indian attended to her and not the others?

Just then the man lifted Nellie off her feet and hoisted her over his shoulder.

"No!" cried her mother as she jumped up to rescue her daughter. "No!"

The man turned to Nellie's mother, almost snarling at her.

"Sit, Mama!" yelled Nellie. She watched her mother put her fist tightly to her mouth as tears filled her eyes.

The Indian carried Nellie over to a large rock away from the other captives and set her down.

Surprised by this action, Nellie looked up at him and found him smiling. He stooped down and patted her feet. "You can walk again."

Nellie was surprised to hear so many English words. "May I go back to my mother?" she asked innocently.

"No! You stay with me," he answered firmly. "My name is Ki-on-twog-ky, Cornplanter, war chief of the Senecas, Keepers of the Western Gate."

Nellie knew now that these Indians were a long way from home, out of their hunting territory. She had never met a Seneca before, but she knew they were part of the Iroquois nation. The Iroquois who lived near her cabin had been friends with her family. Something must be seriously wrong. Maybe this had to do with the trouble within the Indian nation that her father had talked about.

"My name is Nellie, Nellie Lytle. Can you say that?"

"Nellie is not a good name," said the man with a strange smile.

"I like my name very much," returned Nellie. "May I go back to my mother now?"

"No!"

Angrily Nellie shook her fist. "I want to go

back to my mother. What are you doing with us? Why did you take us so far from home?"

"I fix your feet, little sister. Now you can walk farther towards the setting sun."

"I don't want to walk farther. I want to go home."

The man grabbed Nellie by the shoulders and gave her a quick jerk. "You must walk, little sister. You hear my words."

Nellie knew he was serious. Quickly he lifted her to his shoulder and carried her back to her mother, plopping her on the ground.

"What did he say? What did he want?" questioned her mother.

"I don't know. His name is Cornplanter, and he said he didn't like my name. He said it wasn't a good name."

"What does he know!" blurted Robert. "I like your name."

"I don't know what he is up to, but he has taken a liking to you. That might be good. Be careful not to insult him. He might not offer to help you the next time," Nellie's mother advised.

All around them people huddled in fear. Some of them wept. The same question lay heavy on

everyone's mind — what was going to happen
next?

Nellie now realized that many of the Indians
had left, and only a few young men remained to
guard them. If only Papa would come with help,
she thought to herself. They could easily overcome
these young men. But then she remembered her
mother's words. It might be days or weeks before
she would see her father again. The best they could
do was to stay together and pray for the time they
would be ransomed.

Soon the men who had disappeared returned to
the captives and gave directions to the young
guards. The guards then proceeded to pull the captives to their feet, cut their bonds, and put them
into various groups.

Nellie and her mother and brother held on to
each other, trying to make their own group. But a
tall man with red and black stripes on his face
grabbed for Mrs. Lytle, pulling her away from her
children.

"Mother," screamed Nellie.

Cornplanter, noticing what was taking place,
came over to Mrs. Lytle and escorted her back to
her children. He stood straight as a tree. His thick

black hair was pulled back tightly from his face, making him look fierce.

The two Indians who had raided the Lytle farm and stolen Nellie and Robert now came over and addressed Cornplanter in sharp voices. Although Nellie thought she saw anger in his eyes, Cornplanter spoke calmly, but firmly, in a language unknown to the Lytles.

The man who had led Nellie through the forest so roughly the day before pulled his knife from his sheath. He walked slowly around Cornplanter, speaking harsh words when he stood in front of him. Then he threw his knife between Cornplanter's feet so that the blade buried itself in the ground.

Cornplanter smiled at his adversary, showing that he had no fear of him.

The eyes of the Indian flared with rage, but Cornplanter spoke in a calm voice that seemed to soothe the situation. The man replied in less angry tones and then turned and pulled Nellie's mother to him. Cornplanter took hold of Nellie's arm and reached for Robert.

"No!" cried Nellie, remembering her mother's words. "He must stay with my mother."

Robert stood silently beside Nellie and looked at his mother. Tears rolled down his cheeks.

Nellie touched Cornplanter's arm as she stood between him and her captors. "Please, please," she said as she pushed Robert towards her mother. "He stays with Mama, please."

Cornplanter picked up Robert and handed him to Mrs. Lytle. Together she and Robert sobbed as the war chief led Nellie away into the wilderness.

Nellie turned back briefly to see her mother and brother forced in the opposite direction by the two Indians who had stolen them only yesterday. She heard her mother call, "Have courage, my daughter. We will all be home together one day."

More fearful than ever, Nellie followed Cornplanter into the forest. Where were they going? How would her father ever find her now that she was separated from the other captives?

Nellie watched the wilderness around her, making note of the streams they crossed and the places that looked different than the rest of the landscape. Perhaps if she could escape, she thought, she could find her way back to Papa and help him find her mother and Robert.

Nellie followed Cornplanter the entire day. He

walked slowly so that she could keep up. Once he
stopped and washed her feet in a cold stream,
applying more ointment and then rewrapping them
in the bandages. Only once, however, did he try to
make conversation. Nellie thought he seemed sad.

When evening came Nellie was so tired she
could barely stay awake. Although she had been
thankful that her wrists weren't tied, she now
began to feel that the giant man might have to
lead and drag her if they were to continue the journey. Occasionally he allowed her to rest, but each
time it was more painful to move again.

Darkness filled the woods and Nellie's
thoughts returned to her mother and Robert. How
she wished they were with her. So far Cornplanter
was far kinder than the other warriors. She shook
with emotion as she imagined her family on a
wilderness trail, moving farther and farther from
her.

Through the night the pair walked and rested,
walked and rested. Just before dawn the man
stopped, brought his hands to his mouth, and made
the sound of an owl hooting. All was silent in the
forest except for a light wind that brought some
early autumn leaves down upon them. Again,

Cornplanter gave his call. This time, however, came the answer of another owl.

Within minutes Nellie and the Indian were surrounded by men who seemed to come silently with the early daylight. Cornplanter was home.

Chapter 5
The Village

The braves that surrounded Cornplanter laughed
and chattered, happy to see him return home
safely. They spoke between themselves and slapped
each other on the back. They seem to be good
friends, Nellie thought.

Soon the Indians' attention turned to Nellie. As
they looked into her face, Nellie boldly studied
them, noticing that they wore no war paint.
Several of the men tugged at her hair as if they
had never seen that hair color before. One yanked
his knife from its sheath and tried to cut a handful.
Before he managed to do so, Cornplanter pushed
him away and spoke to him harshly.

Nellie breathed a sigh of relief, both hating her
captor and feeling grateful to him.

Cornplanter threw her over his shoulder as he
walked out of the forest and into an open area.
Nellie looked around in surprise. Here was a cornfield in the deep wilderness. The tall tasseled
plants swished back and forth and grazed her face
as she dangled over Cornplanter's shoulder. The
smell of wood smoke filled her nostrils, and she

could hear dogs barking in the distance. We must be near a village, thought Nellie.

Cornplanter slowed his pace and swung Nellie to the ground. Before them stood a palisade which surrounded the village. This giant fence was made of poles ten to fifteen feet high, their tops sharpened to a point. Through the cracks Nellie could see flames from campfires.

Nellie felt herself begin to shake with fear. She had heard stories of how captives were made to run a gauntlet when they arrived at a village. Villagers with sticks and rocks would line the entry way and try to hit the captives as they ran by. If captives could endure the ordeal, they were welcomed into the village.

From inside the palisade Nellie could hear voices calling to Cornplanter. As the gates opened she saw two rows of people holding sticks and other objects, including a pumpkin. Instantly she knew that this was the gauntlet, the corridor of people she must run through to survive.

In panic, Nellie turned and darted towards the cornfield. Her escape lasted only seconds as Cornplanter grabbed hold of her long hair and used it like a leash to pull her back to his side.

The Indians laughed at her failed escape, while
Cornplanter held both her arms in his steel grip.
In a quiet voice he said, "Do not be afraid. Have
courage."

Tears burned Nellie's cheeks. Have courage.
Wasn't that what her mother had also told her?

Cornplanter took Nellie's hand in his and
together they walked through the gates. The
villagers yelled and cheered as the pair grew
closer. Cornplanter, happy at this reception, smiled
and nodded. Then in a loud clear voice he spoke to
them. Although Nellie could not understand, she
guessed he was telling them how they had taken
many prisoners.

Finally Cornplanter ended his speech and
turned to Nellie. The crowd was silent as he raised
his hand above her head. This time he spoke
briefly, and then touched her head in a gentle way.
The crowd gave a cheer, and Nellie noticed that
some quickly broke away, taking their weapons
with them. What had he said to stop the gauntlet?
Nellie wasn't sure, but she was grateful.

As Cornplanter guided her through the crowd,
the frightened Nellie tried to move quickly. But
those she passed laid their hands on her. They

tugged at her hair, grabbed and pinched her arms, and pulled at her skirts. Faces closed in around her, but she avoided their stares. Some of the villagers, however, reached out and patted her kindly.

At the end of the procession Cornplanter led her through the village. In her whole life Nellie had never been in a village that had so many people. There were sounds and smells she had never experienced. Most of the houses were long with rounded roofs. Slabs of bark covered their pole frames. She knew the Iroquois were sometimes called the People of the Longhouse because of these homes. There were a few buildings, however, that had a shape similar to her family's cabin.

It was clear to Nellie that Cornplanter was a powerful and honored man among his people. Those who had not gathered at the gate stood beside their skin-covered doorways and welcomed him home.

Cornplanter came to a stop before a large lodge. Pulling aside a blanket that covered the door, he directed her into the longhouse and stooped to enter it himself. In the dim light Nellie could see three fires in the center aisle of the house, one for each of the families who lived here.

As they moved towards the far end of the lodge, Nellie saw an old woman sitting silently on a mat. The woman was wrapped in a blanket, and her long gray hair hung nearly to the ground. Her face was streaked with black, and she seemed to be in a daze.

Cornplanter knelt beside the woman and gently put his hand on her shoulder. Slowly she turned her attention to him. A toothless smile broke across her face, and she reached out her arms to encircle his neck.

After his welcome, Cornplanter stood up and pointed to Nellie. He motioned for Nellie and at the same time began talking to the old woman. With tears in her eyes, the old woman put her hands out to Nellie. Sensing that she would be expected to do the same, Nellie stepped forward and put out her hands. The woman took them and pulled Nellie down into her lap. Taking Nellie's face in her hands, she brought it to hers so that their foreheads touched.

Nellie wanted desperately to pull away from the woman, but did not dare. Then she felt Cornplanter's hand on her shoulder. "This is my mother, Old Queen. She is now your mother and will take care of you as you will take care of her."

Nellie looked up at Cornplanter. "I already have a mother," she protested.

"This is a new mother. You are my sister. Today you eat and rest. Tomorrow will be a new life for you."

Nellie sat unhappily by the old woman and wondered what Cornplanter meant. The old woman handed her a bowl of hot fish soup from a kettle that hung over the fire. Suddenly Nellie remembered how hungry she was, and she ate greedily.

Cornplanter sat and ate with Nellie and the old woman. In other parts of the longhouse Nellie could see people watching them. She wondered what they thought of her — if they were judging her.

When Cornplanter finished his soup, he stepped over to a small platform along the wall. "Sleep here, sister. This will be your place. It was once my brother's. He was killed six moons ago by Lanape, my enemy. You now are my brother and sister."

Just then a woman approached them with a steaming bowl of meat. She knelt beside

Cornplanter and offered him food. Cornplanter did
not seem surprised but calmly reached into the
bowl and pulled out a large turkey leg. He paused,
and then handed it to Nellie.

Although Nellie was full, she knew she must
accept his offer. She took the greasy leg in her
hand, took a deep breath, and put it to her mouth.
At the same moment the woman, who seemed
offended by Cornplanter's gift to Nellie, started to
snatch the leg away from her. Cornplanter knocked
the woman's hand aside and spoke to her in harsh
tones. The woman, now more upset than before,
glared at Nellie.

Not sure what to do, Nellie looked to
Cornplanter for directions.

"This is my woman. She does not want you for
my sister. You will take her place at my mother's
fire. You are now my mother's daughter and most
favored," explained Cornplanter.

"Eat," he said as he took another turkey leg
from the bowl and passed it to his mother.

With a sick feeling in her stomach, Nellie
slowly took a bite of meat. Its greasy skin hung
loose, and its juices ran down her chin.

Soon Cornplanter's wife stood, taking her bowl

and passing it to several others who were in the
lodge. Cornplanter called to her and seemed to
direct her to the second fire. Cornplanter stood as
if to follow her. Before he left, however, he spoke to
his mother and pointed to Nellie's feet. He pulled
off her moccasins and unwrapped the dirty bandages. Nellie could see that her wounds were heal-
ing, even though her feet were still swollen and
sore.

The old woman nodded and patted her son.
Then she reached into a pile of blankets beside her
and pulled out a leather bundle. As she opened it
Nellie saw dried leaves and blossoms along with
several leaf packages like the one in Cornplanter's
pouch. Cornplanter and his mother spoke briefly,
and then she motioned him to leave and join his
wife. With a smile and a few gentle words, he left.

For the first time since Nellie had arrived, the
old woman rose to her feet, her shoulders bent
with age. Rummaging through her belongings, she
brought out a bark container and filled it with
steaming water from a kettle on the fire. Then she
crushed some leaves from her leather bundle and
stirred them in the water.

The familiar smell of medicine filled the air,

and Nellie knew it was time for her feet to be stewed once again. But the woman took a bladder of drinking water and poured some into the bark container. Carefully she stuck a finger into the brew and tested its temperature. She had cooled the water for Nellie. With a smile and a kind voice she spoke in words Nellie did not understand.

Nellie put down the turkey leg and scooted her feet into the concoction, soaking away the pain inflicted upon her during her days of travel. The food and warm water made her realize just how tired she was. She fought to stay awake as the old woman dried her feet, applied a thick smelly ointment, and wrapped them with cloth.

When the old woman's duty was complete, she pointed to the platform that Cornplanter said would now be Nellie's. Nellie nodded gratefully and made her way to the bed while the old woman smiled with satisfaction.

Nellie slept for long periods through the remainder of the day and then through the night. When she finally awoke the next morning, she could see streaks of sunlight peeking through the cracks in the bark that covered the lodge. Outside she could hear the voices of adults and children already at work and play. There was a whiff of roasted meat in the air.

As she started to sit up Nellie noticed a large brown spider had created a cage for her between two poles above her. The spider lay in wait for a captive right over her face.

For a moment Nellie watched the spider on its lacy web. Then suddenly two hands reached out and snatched it, breaking the threads. Nellie sat up with a start, her face pushing into what remained of the webbed netting. Sticky invisible strands stuck to her nose and lips.

A boy about her size stood beside her and played with the spider, letting it run from one hand to the other. He laughed and spoke in a language Nellie could not understand. Soon he placed the spider carefully on the lodge wall and watched as it raced away.

"Bonsho," said the boy to Nellie, nodding his head in greeting. "Bonsho."

Just then Nellie heard a call, and the boy turned and ran back to the fire near the entrance of the longhouse.

He must mean *bonjour*, thought Nellie. He probably knows some French words from fur traders. She, too, knew some of the expressions of the Frenchies, as Robert always called them.

Nellie looked around her and examined the longhouse more seriously than she had done the previous day. This had the right name, she thought. The lodge was about sixty feet long and almost half as wide. There were three fires and three holes in the roof for the smoke to escape. Platforms used for beds lined the lower walls while shelves used for storing goods lined the walls above them. Mats and animal hides covered much of the hard-packed floor. Cooking odors and the smell of fires, Indian tobacco, and dogs filled the air.

Nellie was alone in the longhouse. She noticed how neatly the old woman had stored her belongings under the sleeping platforms or on the shelves. She also had various bags and bundles hanging on the wall. Everything is in its place, thought Nellie, just like home.

The thought of home made Nellie's stomach feel uneasy. Where were Mama, Papa, Robert, Meggie, and Tommy now? She felt tears welling up in her eyes, and she bit down hard on her bottom lip. She must be brave and strong she told herself, no matter how long it would be until she saw them again.

Resolving never to go anywhere again without shoes, Nellie reached for her moccasins. She had just slipped her foot into one when she felt something wiggling around inside. Startled, she yanked it off and threw it down.

From behind a screen near the head of her bed she heard laughter. She turned to find the boy who had rescued the spider now holding a small gray mouse by its tail. Nellie began to laugh, momentarily forgetting her loneliness and fear.

"Moose in moccasin," laughed the boy. Then he repeated, "moose," shaking the tiny creature by the tail.

"You mean 'mouse'," Nellie corrected.

"*Oui*, moose, mouse," he grinned.

"You speak English?"

"*Oui* and *Francais*. Ki-on-twog-ky — Cornplanter, my uncle — teach me. He is a great man. He learned from English and Frenchie."

The boy stood and played with the tiny mouse as it crawled between his fingers trying to escape.

"You want it?" he asked Nellie. "Don't let Old Queen see. She will put it in cook pot. Moose-mouse eats corn and makes Old Queen mad."

"Maybe you should let it go," said Nellie who did not really want a pet mouse and did not like the idea of holding it captive.

"Maybe it came to keep you company, teach you lessons."

"How can a mouse teach lessons?" asked Nellie.

"You learn from everything — rocks, plants, animals. Animals are four-legged brothers."

Nellie remembered hearing this from Robert's friend, Little Bear. Maybe all Indians believe this, she thought.

"Old Queen meets with Clan Mothers. Cornplanter's wife tried to turn Clan Mothers against you. You are not welcome by her. She is like crazy animal. Everyone says so. Old Queen, *trés bien*. She will take care of any problem with Clan Mothers. She will take good care of you."

Nellie wondered what all this meant. If she wasn't wanted by Cornplanter's wife, why would Cornplanter bring her here?

"What is your name?" she finally asked the boy.

The boy smiled. "Name Hai-wa-ye-is-tah, one who always does right."

"I like that name. Do you always do right?"

"My mother thinks so," smiled Hai-wa-ye-is-tah.

"I wish my mother thought I always did right. My name is Eleanor Lytle, but everyone calls me Nellie."

"That is no good name. What means Nellie?"

Nellie looked hurt and puzzled.

"Names need meaning. Cornplanter is tall and strong like growing corn. He provides for his people and grows a village. Old Queen calls him 'Big White Man' because his father was pale like you."

"Nellie is not good name. Not good on tongue. You need new name."

Nellie had had enough of this conversation. She knew now that the boy did not always do right, because he had made her very cross. She picked up her moccasins and slipped them onto her feet. Standing with her fists clenched she stomped, "I like my name. It has meaning. It means ME!"

Just then many women entered the far end of the lodge. "It is time," Hia-wa-ye-ish-ta said and ran off still holding the mouse.

The women proceeded to the section of the lodge where Nellie stood, and the Old Queen

motioned the girl to come to her. The Old Queen
held a large flat rock with something on it that
looked to Nellie like dried and twisted grass. One
of the women lit the grass from the fire, and soon a
sweet smell filled the longhouse. Using a hawk's
wing the Old Queen fanned the sweet smoke onto
Nellie, from the top of her head to her feet.

A dozen women circled Nellie and sang as the
Old Queen continued to fan the sweet smoke.
Cornplanter's wife stood beside the old woman.
Nellie thought she saw anger in the younger
woman's eyes. Why am I more favored than her?
Nellie wondered as she tried to make sense of what
Cornplanter had told her.

The women and the Old Queen made their way
out of the longhouse with Nellie a part of their procession. People gathered as they walked by and
sang with them. The song was sad and slow, Nellie
thought, like a funeral procession. The women
hung their heads, and some cried.

The parade of women went out the gates of the
village and along the edge of the cornfield. There
they passed other women who sat on platforms and
protected the corn from wild animals and birds.
The parade continued to the banks of a small, deep

river near the village and stopped. Nellie could feel her heart pounding in her chest. What was to happen?

One of the women entered the water and motioned Nellie to follow. Cornplanter's wife pulled at Nellie's clothes, ripping her chemise as she tried to remove it. "No!" cried Nellie, frantically pulling away. She balled her fists and tried to fight the tears that began rolling down her face.

The Old Queen stepped up to Nellie and spoke to her in words she could not understand. Then she handed the burning incense to another woman and walked to the water's edge. There she unknotted the shoulder ties of her loose dress, dropped it to the ground, and proceeded into the water. Nellie was surprised to see that the black paint that covered her face also covered her body.

Quickly the Old Queen submerged herself in the deep stream. She scrubbed her face and body over and over again with sand from the river bottom. When she had finally removed the paint, the Old Queen smiled and emerged from the river, her long hair dripping. On the shore the women sang a kind of chant, fluttering their tongues against their upper lips. Nellie noted that the chant was much happier than their procession song had been. Some younger women had taken the Old Queen's dress and brought a new one which they now helped her put on.

The Old Queen offered her hand to Nellie, who now understood it was her turn to wash in the river. Cornplanter's wife again pulled at Nellie's skirts.

"No! I will do it myself!" Nellie shouted stubbornly. The old woman smiled as Nellie took her garments off and plunged into the river. Cornplanter's wife followed her in and began to wash Nellie's hair, dunking her head under the water in a rough manner. Another woman rubbed Nellie with sand and soft plants from the river's edge.

When they had finished, Nellie's skin was a bright pink. The women on the bank began singing again. At the water's edge the Old Queen held out a long shirt-like dress similar to the ones the women wore. She helped Nellie put it on and knotted a woven belt around her waist. Then she placed a new pair of moccasins decorated with porcupine quills at Nellie's feet. The women clucked their tongues and continued to make noise.

Nellie noticed that Cornplanter's wife went to the bank of the river where Nellie had dropped her clothes. "I want my clothes," Nellie insisted as she pointed.

The Old Queen took the clothes from the younger woman and handed Nellie her skirt. She handed Cornplanter's wife the chemise she had ripped. The younger woman gave the Old Queen a hateful stare.

The women led Nellie back to the village, singing happy songs. Cornplanter and others met them at the gates. Hoisting Nellie onto his shoulder he called out something in a great booming voice. "I have announced," he told Nellie, "that you are now my sister."

Chapter 6
Gro-we-na

To celebrate the addition to Cornplanter's family, the villagers prepared a feast. Several women roasted a deer on a spit. Others prepared soup in large kettles. The food was shared by everyone except Cornplanter's wife. Nellie noticed she was absent and wondered how long the woman would remain angry.

Nellie sat beside the Old Queen and ate until she could hold no more. Although she felt remarkably content with these people, she was still confused about what had happened that morning. Cornplanter had explained that his mother had washed away the grief of her son's death. Nellie herself, he said, had washed away her old blood and had been reborn from the river as his sister.

Now Nellie sat puzzled. None of this made sense. How had she washed away her blood?

Hai-wa-ye-is-tah pushed into the circle where Nellie sat. He held a small bark box. "For you," he said and opened the lid so that his new friend could peer in at the gift. There was the little gray mouse.

Nellie smiled. "Thank you; *merci*. This is a nice gift."

Hai-wa-ye-is-tah beamed with pride. "I made the box. Today you and your family must have gifts."

"Gifts? I don't understand."

"For birth."

"My birth?" ventured Nellie, afraid what the answer might be.

"*Oui*. You are the Old Queen's daughter. Women washed you in the river; gave you new clothes. You have a new life. You are Seneca now. You are pure like my people."

"You can't wash away someone's blood."

"You are Seneca," insisted Hai-wa-ye-is-tah. "Pure."

"I am not!" retorted Nellie as she sprang to her feet and made her hands into fists. Standing nose-to-nose with Hai-wa-ye-is-tah, she pushed him and stomped her feet. The Indians nearby laughed as Nellie knocked the boy off balance.

Cornplanter rose to his feet and stood beside them.

"I am not a Seneca, and you are not my family," she protested to Cornplanter, positioning her feet firmly in front of him.

Cornplanter smiled. "You are my little sister now. Forever."

"I already have brothers, and you are too old to be my brother," Nellie continued defiantly. "And she is too old to be my mother!" Nellie pointed to the Old Queen. "I just want to go home!" cried Nellie as she stomped her feet again.

"Little Sister," Cornplanter argued, "you are home."

An old woman who was sitting close to the Old Queen leaned forward and whispered in her ear. The Old Queen laughed and turned to her neighbor. Soon the whisper made its way around the fire with everyone sharing the joke except Cornplanter and Nellie.

Cornplanter noticed the commotion and stopped Nellie's protests by shaking her lightly by the shoulder. The Old Queen put her hands out and in a loud voice said, "Gro-we-na."

A smile broke over Cornplanter's face. "Ahh, Gro-we-na," he said and nodded in approval. Everyone laughed and cheered.

Not knowing what was going on, Nellie turned angrily to her left and then to her right. "Why are you laughing? What are you saying?"

"You want to know what they say? You ask me,
one who is not your brother?" Cornplanter folded
his arms across his chest and looked down at
Nellie.

Nellie hung her head, not knowing whether
she should be mad or ashamed.

Cornplanter bent over and took Nellie's hands
in his. "They laugh because they have found a
name for my little sister. Gro-we-na, they call you."

"What does that mean, 'Gro-we-na'?"

"'Little Ship Under Full Sail.' You are full of
wind, sure of your direction, and not easily stopped
or turned — like the great vessels that belong to
white people. You move ahead like a little ship
under full sail."

Nellie, who did not want a new life or a new
family, definitely did not want a new name — especially one like Gro-we-na. She sat down, defeated.
She did not speak. She had lost the battle. She had
no choice but to accept. Now all she could do was to
wait for her father to rescue her from these people.
She would never answer to Gro-we-na, never. "I am
Nellie," she said quietly, as if to herself. "I am
Nellie Eleanor Lytle."

Hai-wa-ye-is-tah knelt down beside Nellie. Touching her on the shoulder, he handed her the bark box. "Your name is good," he said. "It means something."

Hanging her head in dismay, Nellie watched as family after family brought gifts to their circle — a blue blanket, red beads, woven belts, moccasins, a roll of ribbon, a bolt of cloth. Cornplanter ate and laughed with his friends, and the Old Queen smiled in delight as she examined the gifts.

Cornplanter's wife, who had now joined the party, picked up the red beads and placed them around her neck. The Old Queen called out harshly, instructing her to put them back on the pile. She pointed to Nellie, indicating that the gifts belonged to her new daughter Gro-we-na. Embarrassed and shamed, Cornplanter's wife pulled the beads from around her neck and tossed them back onto the pile. She glared now at her new sister. The look gave Nellie the chills. She knew she would have to be careful around this woman, who rose and disappeared into the shadows of the lodge.

Around the fires women and children danced and sang to the beat of drums. It had been a hard

day for Nellie, and the evening sky turned her
thoughts to home. She tried to imagine that Pa
had found Meggie and Tommy, that Mama and
Robert had already been ransomed, and that they
all might be dancing to Papa's fiddle as he played
in front of the fire.

Or were her brothers and sister around other
Indian fires, becoming part of other families? She
thought again of her mother's words, "Be strong
and have courage."

Chapter 7
Gray Mouse

The next morning the sun shone brightly, and the young women left their lodges to work in the fields. Harvest time was nearing, when vegetables needed to be picked and prepared for winter storage. The men of the village were busy hunting and fishing. Pole frames lined the village streets as women dried the meat and fish the men already had brought home.

Nellie went with the women to work in the fields. She was given plenty of freedom, but she knew that she was too far from any frontier settlement to escape. Nellie also noticed that someone always worked near her, watching her closely.

The women worked hard, but they shared songs and stories that helped make the time go by quickly. Some of the younger women brought their babies on cradleboards and hung them in trees. The breeze swayed the boards back and forth, keeping the babies content while their mothers worked. Toddlers stayed at their mothers' side, and several times Nellie saw women explaining something about a plant or insect the children brought to them. She noticed how well everyone worked together and how happy they seemed about the harvest.

Nellie remembered the winter before her capture. Her father had said it was the hardest he had ever seen. They had barely enough food to make it until spring, and so she understood how important it was to store plenty of food for the winter months.

During the busy work day Nellie had no time to worry about her family or to wonder if she would soon be ransomed. The women treated her with kindness. Some tried to teach her the Indian names of different vegetables, and Nellie tried to teach them how to say "Nellie." They just shook their heads and laughed, repeating the name "Growe-na" and pointing at her in a teasing manner. Nellie kept her distance from Cornplanter's wife, who also seemed to avoid her.

As the workday ended a woman who seemed to be in charge escorted her back to her lodge. She spoke to the Old Queen as if she was reporting on Nellie's work. The Old Queen glowed with pride and that evening gave her new daughter the red beads that Cornplanter's wife had admired.

This was the first time Nellie had received

such a beautiful gift. The glass beads lined a string
of sinew and hung down long and heavy on her
neck.

She could not believe the beads now belonged
to her!

That night when the Old Queen was elsewhere
Nellie brought out the box with her mouse. She fed
it pieces of corn biscuits the Old Queen had made
and dripped water from her fingers so that it could
drink. She also placed some twigs and leaves in the
box. Nellie knew this gift was not one she would
keep. She would turn the mouse loose, because like
her, it was a captive.

The next morning Nellie wore the beads when
she returned to the fields. She was proud that her
work had been good enough to receive a gift from
the Old Queen. She was also pleased when the
young women admired the beads.

Today Cornplanter's wife did not ignore her.
Instead she worked near Nellie whenever possible.
Several times when Nellie's back was turned she
threw clods of dirt at her. Nellie tried to ignore her.
It seemed like silly behavior for a grown woman,
but Nellie was unsure what to do about the situation.

As the days went by, Nellie was more and more aware of her important status as the Old Queen's daughter. She was both grateful to her Indian mother and Cornplanter, and angry that she was their captive. She had been stolen from her home and brought to this place, far from her real family.

Now Nellie had to do as her mother said — survive. She thought of her mother's instructions each time someone called her 'Gro-we-na,' the name she still detested. She thought about it each time a clump of dirt flew across the rows of vegetables and slapped her on the back.

One afternoon Nellie was called to help weed a squash patch. After working hard for a long period, she decided to carry the weeds out of the patch and get a cool drink from a water bladder that hung on a shade tree.

Nellie picked up her large bundle of weeds and made her way through the garden, careful not to bump the other workers or children. The sun was warm and Nellie thought about how good the water would taste. Just as she began to move more quickly she tripped over something, skinning her knee and elbow as she hit the ground.

Shocked and surprised, Nellie soon felt the

sting from her wounds. Several women nearby
came to help, except Cornplanter's wife who smiled
at Nellie and turned back to her work.

SHE tripped me! Nellie thought to herself.
Fighting mad, she jumped to her feet and yelled,
"She tripped me! She did it on purpose! She
tripped me!"

The women around Nellie tried to calm her,
but without success. Cornplanter's wife continued
her work, ignoring the outburst.

Nellie could not be stopped. She dove at the
woman, crushing squash plants in her path. The
woman fought back viciously, clawing and tearing
at the young girl. In the struggle Nellie's necklace
broke, and the red beads spilled into the plants
and weeds. Quickly the other women pulled the
two apart, laughing at Cornplanter's wife whose
hair was pulled from its braid and hung in her
face. Then they scurried to retrieve Nellie's beads,
which disappeared into dirty hands and pockets.

The anger still raged inside Nellie as she
walked back to the longhouse with her bloody
elbow and knee. She was sure she had never met
anyone so evil in all her life. It was her fault that
Nellie's beautiful beads were gone. It was her fault

that Nellie's elbow and knee were bleeding. But what was she going to do about this woman? She was Cornplanter's wife. She was the Old Queen's daughter-in-law.

When Nellie arrived at the lodge everyone was gone. She cleaned her wounds and lay on her bed. As she continued to nurse her anger, she heard the scratching of the little mouse in his box.

Nellie snatched the box and lifted its lid. The little gray creature twitched its pink nose at her and wiggled its whiskers. Its black eyes, shiny and deep, seemed to tell her that it longed to be free.

"Gro-we-na?" whispered a voice. "Gro-we-na, bosho." It was Hai-wa-ye-is-tah. "You are brave to fight with an enemy who lives so near."

Nellie hadn't thought about that. "You heard?" she asked.

The boy nodded. "Did the mouse talk to you?"

Nellie smiled, knowing the boy had been watching her. "I think he did. He wants to be free. He wants to go home to his mama and papa and brothers and sister." Nellie could feel the tears coming to her eyes.

"You speak very good mouse to know all that.

"Did mouse also tell you his story?" he continued "You listen. I will tell you a story I have heard many times. It is the lesson of the mouse."

Nellie sat up as Hai-wa-ye-is-tah settled down beside her. "May I call you Hai-wa? Your name is so long."

The boy nodded and smiled. "But I will call you Gro-we-na, and you will not be full of anger for me, *oui?*"

Nellie agreed.

"The story of Gray Mouse is like you," Hai-wa began. "He was always certain of his own way and went out for a walk alone. He was warned not to do this, but Mouse was full of knowing. He was full of being a fluffy gray mouse who did as he wanted.

"Gray Mouse traveled a long time alone."

"I bet his feet hurt," Nellie interrupted.

"He traveled so far he became lost in the forest. Along the trail he heard a noise. Gray Mouse was afraid. There was no place to hide. He stood frozen in his tracks. Coming through the grass were two black eyes and black mask. It was Raccoon.

"Raccoon said, 'Why are you here alone so far from home?'

"Gray mouse said, 'I am out for a walk.'

"'You are alone and lost, Gray Mouse. Let me be your friend. I will help.'

"'I don't need a friend. I am not lost.'

"'Very well,' said Raccoon. 'I will walk beside you on your way.'

"Gray Mouse and Raccoon walked together on the trail. Mouse would not tell Raccoon, but he was glad to have Raccoon with him.

"As they walked toward the setting sun Gray Mouse heard a roaring thunder. Afraid, he tried to walk under Raccoon for safety. Raccoon had to lift his legs high so not to squash mouse. But Raccoon was not angry. He knew it is hard to admit fear. He knew it best to be kind and help others learn. So Raccoon walked bravely in big steps towards the thunder because he knew it was only the sound of the river.

"When they reached the river, Mouse watched carefully as the water rushed by. He had never seen water so powerful. Gray Mouse learned that there were things on Great Mother Earth that he had not seen before. The river was not like the little creek that ran by his home.

"Raccoon turned from Gray Mouse. 'I leave now. I have fishing to do.'

"'What will become of me now you have led me to this great river?'

"'But I did not lead you,' said Raccoon. 'We only walked together. Besides, my friend Owl will soon be here to keep you company.'

"'Owl? He is my enemy,' cried Mouse.

"'Then make him your friend. And look around you. Smell the air for the way home. Our Great Mother the Earth can tell you many things if you only listen. Filled with your own thoughts, you will never learn and grow. Do you remember the plants and grasses we passed on our way? Did you observe the world around you, or were you too full of yourself to think about these things?' Raccoon gave Mouse a thoughtful look and disappeared along the water's edge.

"Gray Mouse stood shivering with fright and watched the great river. What would he do all alone? He began to think. He remembered how warm the sun was on his fur when he traveled. He remembered the smell of corn and the smell of acorns from the fields and forest. He remembered very well the sound of the river and how it faced the setting sun.

"Soon Owl came to its perch and called down to

Gray Mouse. 'What are you doing here? Ho-ho-who
are you?'

"Gray Mouse said, 'I am Gray Mouse and
Raccoon brought me to this place.'

"'Raccoon? He is a friend, so I will not eat you.
Besides, you are too little and thin for me to waste
my time.'

"With that Gray Mouse was very insulted. 'I
am not little and thin. I am Gray Mouse.'

"'So then I should eat you?' laughed the Owl.

"Gray Mouse put his little whiskers up into the
air, thinking he would hide his anger and fear.

"'What is wrong, Gray Mouse? Are you angry?'

"Gray Mouse could only think of himself. He
was lost, and Owl teased him.

"'If you wish to go home, Gray Mouse, you
must jump into the air so you can see your way
like winged creatures do. You must jump high.'

"Gray Mouse did not want to seem stupid. 'I
know this, Owl,' he said. 'You do not need to help
me.'

"And so Gray Mouse jumped. But he could see
nothing but the tall grass and the river. He jumped
again, only higher. This time he saw lily pads on
the river and turtles swimming. He jumped again

and saw across the river. He saw mountains in the
distance, and he saw the setting sun. He jumped
again, and when he came down he plopped right
into the river and sank to the cold, wet bottom.

"Gray Mouse kicked his feet so hard in his
struggle he forgot all about his anger. He forgot all
about how smart he was, how gray his coat was,
and how he was always right and never needed to
listen. When he forgot all this, he became lighter.
He popped up to the top and pulled himself up onto
Earth.

"Tired and afraid, Gray Mouse cried, and for
the first time he was glad Mother Earth was his
friend.

"Owl called, 'Did you see your way?'

"Gray Mouse was grateful just to be alive and
did not stick his little whiskers in the air. His ears
and tail drooped.

"'I saw many things, Owl, and I learned. I did
not see my way before because my whiskers were
in the way.'

"Owl cocked his head. 'Gray Mouse, it is good
you see things around you as they are. Things
around you are much bigger than you and much
quieter. The sun is there every day, but does not

brag. The mountains are home to many and are very beautiful, but silent. They are not proud. The valley is calling to you. You have to listen. It is your home. You will know its voice.

"'Did you see all these things when you jumped?'

"'Yes.'

"'And you visited the river?'

"'Yes.'

"'Were you not grateful to see the sun when you returned to the surface to breathe the sweet air and to touch the earth?'

"'Oh, yes.'

"'See, Gray Mouse, today you learned something you already knew but were unable to understand. It is time for you to go home and tell your friends and family of your journey.'

"'But I do not know how to get home.'

"'Did you not smell the wind, watch the sun, discover the valley?'

"'Yes.'

"'Did you not follow a path from your village?'

"'Yes.'

"'Then you know the way home.'

"Gray Mouse smiled at Owl and followed the

wind, the grass, and the path back to the valley.
He told his family about the things he had learned
—that his whiskers were always getting in the way
of seeing, and his anger caused him great dangers
in the river. All of this he was happy to tell because
he knew that he would live and grow old in this
wisdom."

Hai-wa finished the story and smiled at Gro-
we-na. She understood now what he had meant by
animals teaching lessons. Maybe her little gray
mouse had come so that Hai-wa could share the
story.

Nellie decided to learn to watch and listen and
put anger away so that maybe one day she could go
home. She scooped the little creature from its bark
box. Together she and Hai-wa walked outside the
walls of the village and turned the mouse loose in
the woods.

Chapter 8
The Feast of the Green Corn

For Nellie the passing of time was difficult.
Autumn came and moved slowly into the long
nights of winter. The harvest they had celebrated
during the Feast of the Green Corn supplied the
villagers with food until the ice broke from the
rivers in spring.

The Old Queen had grown fond of Nellie and
treated her with kindness. She was very proud of
her adopted daughter and boasted that she worked
hard like a true Seneca. Hai-wa often translated
for the Old Queen as she taught Nellie how to prepare the family's favorite meals. Nellie also cleaned
their section of the longhouse and kept the wood
pile stacked full against the cold winter winds.

As time went by Nellie learned to love the Old
Queen and Cornplanter, who spent long hours in
the winter around the fire of his mother and sister.
The three of them often played games and told stories. Gradually Nellie accepted her new life — and
even the name "Gro-we-na."

It seemed to Gro-we-na that Cornplanter's wife
did not hate her as she once had. She sometimes

invited Gro-we-na and the Old Queen to her fire
for hot soup and choice cuts of meat brought back
from a hunt by Cornplanter. Hai-wa and his family
were also invited, since they were relatives of the
Old Queen.

Hai-wa became Gro-we-na's constant friend.
Together they shared stories and laughter. He
taught her the language of the Seneca longhouse,
and before long Gro-we-na found it difficult to
remember the English words she had once spoken.
There was no place for them in her new life.

But Gro-we-na's memories of the little cabin
and her other family did not fade so easily. As she
sat by the lodge fire, her thoughts drifted to an
almost magical place within her heart. She could
see her brothers and sister sitting by their hearth,
roasting chestnuts while her father played the
fiddle. She often craved the taste of her mother's
smooth white bread or longed for the warmth of
the woolen mittens that she had knitted.

Gro-we-na held on to her memories even as a
member of Cornplanter's family. Summer passed
again into fall, and the harvest was celebrated
with another Feast of the Green Corn. It had been
a full year and still there had been no rescue. What

happened to her family remained a mystery to her.

During the year Cornplanter left the village many times to hunt, fight, or attend the great Council Fires of the Iroquois held near Fort Niagara. Upon his return he always brought gifts of food, blankets, and cloth. The family made good use of the gifts, and Gro-we-na slowly stopped wondering if some settlers or traders had lost their lives trying to protect these prizes.

Through the seasons Gro-we-na learned to tan skins, make moccasins, and dry fish and meat on racks for winter storage. Her favorite job, a skill taught her by the Old Queen, was to make baskets and mats with split ashwood and dried grasses.

As Gro-we-na's skill with the Iroquois language grew, so did her knowledge of the Iroquois people. She learned not only about the Seneca, but also about the Mohawk, Cuyuga, Onondaga, Oneida, and Tuscarora. She was amazed to find that the Clan Mothers were the ones who voted and made decisions that were passed on to the war and peace leaders. Even these leaders were selected by the women.

In the late summer of the third year of her captivity, Gro-we-na awoke one morning feeling very

strange. Her bed was damp and clammy. Her head
pounded. One moment she was so hot she wanted
to plunge into the river, and the next moment she
was so cold her teeth chattered. Suddenly Gro-we-
na became aware that people stood by her bed.
There was the Old Queen, Hai-wa and his mother,
and Cornplanter's wife.

"See, my daughter has opened her eyes," the
Old Queen cried as Gro-we-na started to stir. She
washed Gro-we-na's head with a damp cloth and
tried to cool her from the sweat of her fever. The
old woman's face was lined with worry and fatigue.

Hai-wa's mother held a bowl of broth which
she fed to Gro-we-na, while the Old Queen told her
daughter that two days before she was taken by
fits of shaking and had become unconscious. Gro-
we-na was unaware of this, but she quickly understood that she had frightened her family. They
seemed greatly relieved to have her awake and sip-
ping broth.

With Gro-we-na improved, Hai-wa's mother left
the Old Queen's fire to attend to her own family.
The Old Queen, exhausted from two nights without
sleep, was very weary. Cornplanter was away
hunting and knew nothing of his sister's illness,

but his wife had surprised everyone and come to help the Old Queen care for Gro-we-na. Now the woman again surprised everyone by insisting that the Old Queen go to her bed and rest. She said that she would attend to Gro-we-na, who was still too weak to sit up.

The Old Queen was glad to have some rest. She allowed her daughter-in-law to care for Gro-we-na and collapsed into a deep sleep on her bed. Gro-we-na herself soon fell back to sleep, her body exhausted from the illness.

Hai-wa, who had been given the job of helping the Old Queen during Gro-we-na's illness, brought in wood for the fire. He kept an eye on Cornplanter's wife. He did not like this woman or trust her with his friend. But soon his mother, who also needed his help, called him from the fire. Gro-we-na's illness had been hard on everyone in the longhouse, and many chores had been left undone.

Hai-wa was uncertain if he should leave Gro-we-na. Yet he did not want to displease his mother. He promised himself he would return to watch over his friend as soon as he was able.

It was only a short time after Hai-wa had returned to his fire that he saw Cornplanter's wife

leave the lodge. After a few moments, he stepped
out of the lodge himself and saw her leave the
village gate. Staying far enough behind so that she
would not notice him, Hai-wa followed her through
the cornfields to the edge of the forest and watched
as she picked herbs. Next she went to a group of
May apple plants and pulled several up by the
roots. There, in the shadows of the forest, she took
a rock and mashed the herbs with the May apple
roots.

Hai-wa withdrew quietly and rushed back to
the lodge. Fearful of what Cornplanter's wife would
do next, he hid himself near the screen by Gro-we-
na's bed. Although still asleep, Gro-we-na tossed
and turned.

Soon Cornplanter's wife returned with her
mixture. Looking around to see if anyone was
watching, she quickly added it to some steaming
broth from the kettle. She stirred and stirred until
she was sure the broth had absorbed her
concoction.

When she had finished, Cornplanter's wife
went to Gro-we-na's bed and called to her in a
loving manner. "Sister, sister. Wake up and have
some broth." She held out a small container for

Gro-we-na.

Gro-we-na's eyes slowly opened. The broth
smelled good to her. But as she became more fully
awake she saw Hai-wa standing quietly behind
Cornplanter's wife and shaking his head. His eyes
and face carried an expression of danger that Gro-
we-na understood, even in her weakened state.

Not realizing that Hai-wa was behind her,
Cornplanter's wife continued to urge Gro-we-na to
take the soup. "Sister, look. I have made a broth
that will drive away your illness forever. You must
drink."

Hai-wa stiffened with fear, afraid that Gro-we-
na had not understood his message.

Gro-we-na closed her eyes. "Put it down, my
brother's wife. I will drink the broth later when I
am more fully awake."

Relieved, Hai-wa made his presence known.
"You have made a broth for Gro-we-na. It is right
that she should wait for a time so that she can
enjoy its taste."

The woman turned, startled by the young spy.
"What are you doing here? Do you not have chores
to do?" she asked in an angry tone.

"No, I have decided I will help watch over Gro-we-na today until the Old Queen awakes."

Not wanting to draw suspicion, Cornplanter's wife placed the container of broth beside Gro-we-na's bed. She busied herself around the fire for a short time and then left.

The moment the woman left the longhouse, Hai-wa knelt beside Gro-we-na and shook her until she opened her eyes. "Do not drink what she has brought you. I watched her gather poisonous herbs for this broth. She means to rid herself of you today."

Hai-wa snatched the container and took it to the Old Queen's bedside. After waking her he explained how Cornplanter's wife had made a mixture of herbs and May apple root. Alarmed and fully awake, the old woman inspected the broth. It was, she confirmed, a poisonous concoction. She quickly went to gather the Clan Mothers. Cornplanter's wife, afraid she had been discovered, went into the forest to hide.

Hai-wa returned to Gro-we-na's side and kept watch over her, bringing her water and soup his mother had prepared. By nightfall the Old Queen returned. She knelt by Gro-we-na and wept. She also called Hai-wa to her side and held him tight.

That night the three of them did not speak of
Cornplanter's wife. Gro-we-na knew something
terrible had happened to her.

Over the next two days there was no mention
of what had happened. Many women came to visit
the Old Queen, but made no conversations with
Gro-we-na. Hai-wa was not allowed to talk with
Gro-we-na either. They were kept apart, even
though the boy would often come and stand near
his friend. He proudly wore a new red wool coat
the Old Queen had given him for saving her
daughter.

On the third day Cornplanter returned.
Outside the lodge there was much commotion. Gro-
we-na was still confined to her bed, but she could
hear many voices and the sounds of people rushing
about. Cornplanter soon came to her side and with
tears in his eyes, he sat and held her hand. She
could not understand why no words were spoken.

That afternoon several women came to
Cornplanter's fire in the lodge and helped him
remove his wife's baskets and clothes. They loaded
their arms and solemnly left with Cornplanter
following.

Gro-we-na was again alone when Hai-wa crept

beside her sleeping pallet and told her all that had
taken place. He told her how the Clan Mothers had
gathered to hear the case against Cornplanter's
wife. The women were angry and debated about
what to do to her. They chose what they believed to
be a terrible punishment — to live without one's
people. And so they banished her, sending her to
live outside of the village walls without protection.
The Clan Mothers forbade that anyone care for her
or speak to her, even her husband or family. She
would be allowed to work alone at the far end of
the cornfield. Hai-wa said that everyone knew in
time that the Great Spirit would decide the
woman's fate.

　　When Gro-we-na was well again she returned
to the field to work and often saw Cornplanter's
wife. Although the other women refused to look at
her, Gro-we-na forgave the banished woman and
felt sorry for her. Cornplanter's wife, however, had
not changed. Each time Gro-we-na was nearby she
struck out at her with her hoe and tried to spit on
her. Gro-we-na learned to harden her heart and
turned away, leaving the woman's care in the
hands of the Great Spirit.

　　It was now the fall of the third year of Gro-we-

na's captivity. It was also time for the Feast of the
Green Corn when everyone gave thanks for the
harvest that would keep them through the long
winter. In previous years Gro-we-na had made special clothes for the celebration, since it was custom-
ary to wear new moccasins, leggings, jackets, or
other items. But this year the Old Queen and
Cornplanter gave Gro-we-na a very special suit of
clothes. They wanted her to look her best at this
year's feast since visitors from other villages would
be there. It was a time for all young Iroquois to
show off their beauty and dream of their future.

As Gro-we-na admired her new clothes, she
recognized the hard work of her family. She
remembered how many times she had watched her
brother go out of the village and trap animals.
When he had many skins he went on a journey and
returned with silver brooches, blue broadcloth, red
wool, and ribbon. These items had been skillfully
employed by the Old Queen and Hai-wa's mother
to make Gro-we-na the most beautiful outfit she
had ever seen.

The Old Queen held out a blue skirt trimmed
with yellow and green ribbons and a long black
blouse decorated with rows of silver brooches.

The women had also made her leggings of
scarlet wool and soft doeskin moccasins embroi-
dered with porcupine quills. Cornplanter gave her
many strings of wampum beads in white and
purple to decorate her neck. He also gave her a
small sack of larger beads that could be woven into
her hair.

Gro-we-na was so surprised by the gifts she
thought she would cry. She truly loved the Old
Queen and Cornplanter. Her brother smiled at his
sister's joy and laughed at the Old Queen who
wept with happiness. They both knew that Gro-we-
na was almost thirteen and that they were
presenting a young woman at the feast who one
day soon would become a bride.

Gro-we-na took her new clothes to her bed and
sat down to inspect the remarkable handiwork.
Hai-wa pointed out which ribbons his mother had
sewn onto the skirt and revealed his jealousy over
her scarlet leggings. Gro-we-na admired the beads
for her hair and thought about the string of red
beads that had been lost long ago in her struggle
with Cornplanter's wife. "These beads tell me I
have grown older and wiser — like Gray Mouse,"
she said to Hai-wa. "They will not be lost like the

others because I cannot see beyond my whiskers."

The next day was the first of the four-day Feast of the Green Corn. In the morning the Old Queen awakened Gro-we-na and brushed and pulled back the girl's hair into a braid, weaving in the large, bright beads. Then Gro-we-na dressed in her new clothes.

When Gro-we-na appeared at the door of the lodge the Old Queen seemed astonished at her daughter's beauty. Cornplanter stood beside his mother, proud of his sister and ready to escort her to the feast.

Gro-we-na's heart beat with excitement. She could hear the drummers beating out rhythms that were now familiar to her. She knew the great dance would be her introduction as a young woman to all the village. There would be others her age who would also enter into the dance circle, but she doubted that they would have leggings of scarlet and beads of wampum like hers.

Just as Gro-we-na and Cornplanter approached the center of the village, a commotion took place. The well-known British Indian agent, Colonial Guy Johnson from Fort Niagara, entered the gate to attend the feast. Three soldiers followed him. Gro-we-na watched as the man in a wig, tall black riding boots, and a blue waistcoat proudly gave the soldiers some orders. His pride and stature reminded her very much of Cornplanter.

Leaving Gro-we-na's side Cornplanter greeted the Colonel and escorted him to the head position at the feasting circle. Gro-we-na entered the girls' dance line and made her way around the drum circle, showing off her new clothes. She soon forgot about Colonel Johnson as she smiled at the young men from nearby villages and giggled and danced with her friends.

Colonel Johnson, however, paid a great deal of attention to Gro-we-na. He noticed that her skin was paler than the rest of the girls, even though she was tanned by the summer sun. He also noticed that her hair was lighter than the other girls and that curls formed around her sweaty face as she danced. She was not Indian, he decided. She must be the American, Eleanor Lytle, the girl her father had sent him to ransom.

All that day Colonel Johnson feasted with Cornplanter and the other chiefs. The officer had brought many gifts with him, hoping to win the heart of the Seneca chief. Cornplanter readily accepted them in exchange for the village's hospitality to Johnson and his men.

The day wore on and was filled with fun for everyone. Johnson waited for his chance to have a council with Cornplanter. At the same time he watched Gro-we-na closely, noting that she seemed to be one of the tribe. There was also a boy constantly at her side. He did not act like a guard, but more like a brother.

When Johnson was sure Cornplanter was content with the celebration, he asked the chief for council.

"This is not a good time, my friend," Cornplanter responded.

"It will never be a good time for what I want to ask you, Cornplanter. I have brought you many gifts and have shared your food. Will you not come with me to speak in council? I have something I must ask you."

Cornplanter, who had no idea what the colonel wanted, was in too good a mood to deny his white friend anything. Colonel Johnson rose to leave the feast and his three men did the same.

"No. They must stay," directed Cornplanter as he motioned to the soldiers to be seated.

Johnson nodded and the two men walked alone
to Cornplanter's lodge. Once inside Cornplanter
filled his pipe with kinick-kinick, lit it, and recited
a prayer. Then he offered the pipe to Johnson.

Johnson had worked with the Iroquois for
years and knew what was expected of him. He took
the pipe from Cornplanter and drew hard on its
long stem. After a few puffs of the Indian tobacco,
he handed it back to Cornplanter who knocked the
unsmoked part of the kinick-kinick into the fire,
making a sweet incense in the air.

When the ritual was over, Colonel Johnson
began. "I see at the dance circle you have many
young women that will be of age by next harvest.
There are many there, and beautiful."

Cornplanter nodded. "Johnson," he asked with
a sly smile, "will you be looking for a new wife?"

"Oh! Heavens no, my friend. I ask only because
I notice one there that is very beautiful and wears
fine things. She has a skirt of blue with scarlet leggings."

Cornplanter knew he spoke of Gro-we-na. "Yes,
she is beautiful and should be ready to wed by next
year. She will marry well as she is my sister Gro-
we-na. The Old Queen has already started to

prepare her to take her place."

"But this Gro-we-na, as you call her, does she not have another name? Is her name not Eleanor Lytle, and is she not a captive from Plum River?"

"She is my sister Gro-we-na. She lives here with my mother. Does she look like a captive? Is she tied with a noose? She is happy. She smiles and dances with her friends. She works in the fields with the women. She is my sister."

"Yes, Cornplanter, and she is also the daughter of Mr. and Mrs. Lytle who now reside at Fort Niagara and have petitioned me to help them get their daughter back. As you know the family was homesteading along the Plum three years ago when an attack on the valley stole away several families. Mrs. Lytle and her little boy Robert were taken and shortly thereafter ransomed. They were reunited with Mr. Lytle and two Lytle children who had escaped the attack. It was Eleanor alone who did not return.

"Her father has spent the last three years trying to track her down. Between his work and mine, we have visited every Iroquois village but yours looking for the girl. And now, here I find her as your sister."

"She is my sister."

"She is also their daughter, Cornplanter. They would give anything you asked to have her back."

"I cannot sell my sister."

"Anything, Cornplanter — silver, guns, riches."

"My sister is not for sale. My heart would break to lose her. You tell me the family has other children. The Old Queen has only Gro-we-na. And she is both sister and brother to me."

"Cornplanter, listen to me. You tell me your heart would break if you had to give her back, so then you know how it is with her parents. Their hearts have been broken for three years, separated from their daughter. Will you not ransom the girl? Will you not let her return to her home where she belongs? Would you have her live her life here in hardship, never really fitting in? You are cruel to your sister if you will let that happen."

Cornplanter, saddened by Colonel Johnson's words, remained silent. He knew what the girl's family felt, for he was now feeling the same hurt.

"I cannot give you my sister."

"Then will you allow her family to visit the girl?"

"It cannot be. My people would not understand."

"Would you let the family visit her at another location? No doubt you will be attending the Great Council soon. Is it not near the Great Falls and Fort Niagara?"

Cornplanter was silent.

"You could bring the girl," Johnson urged. "Her family is there, and we could meet you."

"It is too dangerous. Her family will try to steal her from me."

"No, Cornplanter. I give you my word. I will be there with you and the family. They will do anything just to see their daughter. The mother is near death with worry about the girl. If they are allowed to see her so happy and healthy, so well-dressed, they will know she is in the right place. Their hearts will be at ease, and they will be able to let go of her forever.

"Just this one time, Cornplanter. It is all I ask. You are a wise man and you know these people will be afraid. The Great Council will bring warriors from all over the Iroquois nation. They would never dare to try and steal her from you."

Cornplanter knew what Johnson said was true. There would be more people of the longhouse than the whites could count. "If the family agrees to all that you say," Cornplanter said slowly, "I will bring Gro-we-na to the Great Council. I will tell the Old Queen I am taking the girl to show her young braves from other totems so that she might pick a husband."

"Yes, Cornplanter, that is the thing to do. That way you will not cause your mother needless worry."

As they reached an agreement, Colonel Johnson gave Cornplanter a beautiful silver medallion that hung from a ribbon. "This shows that we have struck a bargain, my friend, and that my word is good."

Cornplanter accepted the gift and led Colonel Johnson to the gate. The soldiers joined their leader as they left the Feast of the Green Corn.

Chapter 9
Reunion at the Great Falls

Gro-we-na watched her brother Cornplanter as he escorted his guest to the village gate. The tall man in his funny white wig looked so different from her people in the village. There are many differences between us, she thought.

When Cornplanter returned to the festivities, Gro-we-na noticed the beautiful silver gorget that hung from her brother's neck. She decided that her brother must have struck some kind of bargain with the wigged man to have been given such a prize.

The Old Queen did not notice her son's medallion. She sat with a group of her friends who ate and laughed as they watched the beautiful young girls dance before the fire circle. She was proud of her daughter and hoped she would catch the attention of the young men who were honorable enough to become chiefs.

Throughout the evening drums, rattles, and jaw harps played, and the fires burned brightly. Gro-we-na was happy to be there with all her friends and family.

The next morning, the second day of the Green
Corn Feast, Gro-we-na asked her mother about the
disk of silver Cornplanter wore around his neck.
"Mother, did you see the beautiful gift the man
from the fort of the Great Falls gave my brother?
Surely my brother must have pleased him with
food and entertainment."

Cornplanter, who sat at the family fire, seemed
not to hear.

"My daughter, there is a time and place for all
things. When your brother wishes to tell his story,
he will tell us both. It is not proper to pry into a
man's business. It is a lesson you have not yet
learned."

Cornplanter knew he would soon have to tell
his sister about his bargain with the Colonel, but
the story would be for her ears alone. Until the trip
to the Great Council, he planned to tell his mother
only that Gro-we-na would accompany him to find
a husband of proper birth and position.

After the Feast of the Green Corn ended,
Cornplanter told his mother about the trip he and
Gro-we-na would take. The Old Woman smiled
with delight, and Cornplanter was slightly more at
ease. It was, after all, partly true. After the meet-

ing with her white people she would have a chance
to meet the sons of chiefs at the Council.

"If Gro-we-na meets the right young man at
the Council, there will be a marriage in our family
before planting time," the Old Queen told
Cornplanter. "Another fire in our longhouse will
warm us all. You, my son, must help your sister
choose well. A strong brave will also be of great
help to you at hunting time."

Cornplanter's heart ached when he heard his
mother speak this way. He hoped all would be so.
He trusted the heart of his sister. He knew that
she had great love for the Old Queen and himself.
But he was unsure of what Gro-we-na's white
family would do. If they dared to steal his sister,
there would be a battle and many women would be
left crying alone at night at their fires and in their
cabins.

As the meeting of the Great Council grew near,
Cornplanter found his sister grinding corn with the
women. Hai-wa was there also, carrying baskets of
corn to their grinding area where his mother
worked beside Gro-we-na.

Gro-we-na sat back on her haunches to rest
when she noticed her brother watching. "My

brother, is it not like a man to watch as the women work so hard?" joked Gro-we-na.

"My sister, it is a great honor for women to grind. It is only the creative powers of women that can bless the grain so it will make food for our people during the freezing time." The women all laughed at the two as they teased one another.

"Gro-we-na, I must speak to you. Please put down your stone and come with me."

Cornplanter had never before bothered her at work. Gro-we-na knew it was something important.

Standing from her place at the grinding stone, she dusted off her hands and followed her brother as he walked through the village gate. Cornplanter was a tall man, and even though she had grown taller in the last few moons, her legs had to stretch to keep up with his pace. "Brother, please wait. Surely your news is not so important as to make your sister run after you."

Cornplanter remained silent and solemn. The two then walked more slowly past the harvest cornfield to the edge of the woods. There Cornplanter sat on a fallen tree and looked up at his sister.

"I have something to tell you, Little Sister. You

must speak only with your heart, as I need to trust your words."

Gro-we-na nodded.

"Do you remember the men from the fort of the Great Falls that came to the Feast of the Green Corn?"

"The man with a wig of white and a coat of blue?" she asked.

"That is the man. I have struck a bargain with this man."

"Is that why you possess the silver gorget?"

Cornplanter shook his head. "He gave me the gift because I listened to his words and because I agreed with him."

"What did you agree about, Brother?"

"It was about you."

Gro-we-na did not understand, but her heart began to pound.

"Do you remember long ago before you were washed in the river and became a Seneca, my sister? Do you remember that time?"

Gro-we-na shook her head. "Those memories are gone now, Brother. I have a new life. I do not want to remember. I am no longer able to speak their tongue."

"That is good, my sister. You have been happy with the Old Queen as your mother?"

"Yes, but please, Brother, you are scaring me."

"Have I not been a good brother for you, little Gro-we-na? Do you not have love in your heart for your family?"

"Yes, yes. Please stop saying these words. I do not know what you mean by all this."

Cornplanter took his sister's hands and held them tightly in his. Looking into her eyes he could see her fear.

"Sister, it is because of all this that I have agreed with Colonel Johnson, the man with the white wig, to take you to his fort."

"I do not want to go to his fort, Brother. Why would I go to his fort? Do you not want me as your sister anymore?" Tears began to run down Gro-we-na's cheeks at the thought of leaving the village.

"It is because another family wishes to visit with you. They are the family you left behind."

Stunned, Gro-we-na did not know what to think about all this. The family she would meet was not her family anymore. She could not remember the words or the faces of those she left behind. Why would they want to see her?

"Gro-we-na, it is because of my love for you that I thought this would be best. Colonel Johnson has promised these people will not try to steal you away. They only want to see that you are well."

"I am well. Couldn't you tell them that? I do not want to see these people," she cried.

"I have given my word."

"You gave your word to receive a gift of silver."

Cornplanter was hurt and angered by his sister's words. "That is not true. I gave my word so these people would not try and come to our village and steal you. If they knew where you were they would surely try. Many people might be hurt — your friends, the Old Queen, and even Hai-wa-ye-is-tah. I did this to keep them safe. I did this because I know your heart is here with us. Once they see your happiness, they will leave you alone. They will leave us all alone."

Gro-we-na, ashamed by her comment, hugged Cornplanter's neck. She knew he would never do anything to hurt her. He had always looked after her. Anything she had ever wanted, anything she had ever needed he made sure she had.

"I am sorry, Brother. You are right. I will do what you ask."

Cornplanter pulled Gro-we-na from his neck. "You must also do something else. Do not tell the Old Queen what I have said. She will be too afraid to let you go. Only tell her you go to seek a husband from the sons of the chiefs."

Gro-we-na smiled. "And after this meeting is over we will attend the Great Council?"

"Yes, my sister, and I will find you a fine young chief to be your husband."

Gro-we-na beamed at this prospect. She knew that this is what she must do.

Cornplanter walked with Gro-we-na back to the grinding place. He knew he could trust her to make the trip and return without telling the Old Queen.

As the days passed the Old Queen packed bundles of food for her children to take to the Great Council. She placed gifts in a bundle for them to give to relatives from the other Seneca villages. She also explained many things to Gro-we-na.

"The Great Council is an important time for the Iroquois people," the Old Queen told her daughter. "Your brother and others will discuss the decisions made by the Clan Mothers and chiefs in each village. They will celebrate the happiness of events and tell of their sorrows. They must also meet with Colonel Johnson and the men of the fort to hear what deals have been struck with the new Government concerning the lands of the Iroquois Nation.

"The great war between the white people has drawn to a close," she continued. "Those who remain in this land call themselves Americans. We, too, have been divided. Many of our people have been killed. Perhaps now the People of the Longhouse can again live in harmony with each other and with the land. I hope this is the message my son brings back with him."

As the time drew near, Gro-we-na tried to show excitement to the Old Queen by constantly talking about those who would attend the Great Council. But inside Gro-we-na was torn by a strange fear and loneliness. One day as she pre-pared for the journey, she found the old skirt she had worn as a child when she was taken from her wilderness cabin. Secretly she took the skirt and walked to the forest's edge. There she sat on a log, trying to remember.

The skirt was very small and very plain and simple. It was not at all like her beautiful Green

Corn dress. As she studied it, she noticed the fine stitches put there by a woman Gro-we-na began to remember. Vaguely she began to see a face in her thoughts, places in her memory. It was the smiling face of a woman with brown hair. Her hair was pulled back as neatly as any Indian woman's. Gro-we-na remembered sitting in the woman's lap and being held close. It was her mother.

Tears welled in Gro-we-na's eyes and rolled down her cheeks. She did remember. It was so long ago, but she did remember. Sobbing, Gro-we-na slid from the tree into the dry grass. "I remember. I remember."

Over the next few days Gro-we-na's memories came flooding back to her. She could see a deep well with a child cranking a bucket of water from it. She could see children playing in a field beside a cabin. She could hear the odd sounds of a musical instrument. There was a man playing, but his face was faded, his name gone.

Gro-we-na kept these memories to herself, knowing that it would upset Cornplanter if he thought she was still tied to someone in her past — someone outside the Seneca village. But at night when she was alone she thought of her brothers and sister, of her mother spinning at her wheel. She remembered the name —Nellie. That was who she once was — Nellie.

Cornplanter carefully watched over his sister as the time for the trip approached. He noticed that she was not her normal, happy self. She was strangely quiet and often sent Hai-wa-ye-is-tah away from her, telling him she wished to be alone. Cornplanter hoped it was Gro-we-na's way of not telling anyone about their real reason for this trip.

The Old Queen thought her daughter was nervous, knowing that she might return with plans to marry. This was a time that would make any young girl more serious and thoughtful. She was about to become a woman and have her own fire, her own family.

On their day of departure Cornplanter helped his sister mount a fine horse. She had packed her best clothes and the bundles the Old Queen had made. The excited Old Queen smiled in assurance. "Be brave, my daughter. Have courage." These were words she had heard before from another mother — her own.

Together Cornplanter and Gro-we-na rode the trail towards Fort Niagara. That night they made

camp high above a fast-moving river, the river that
led to the Great Falls. Gro-we-na had never seen
the Great Falls before, but she had heard stories of
its thundering water. She knew it was a sacred
place, and the Old Queen had even given her a
pouch filled with Indian tobacco to scatter upon the
water near the Council grounds. Had it not been
for the fact she was to meet her old family, the trip
would have been a very happy and exciting time
for Gro-we-na.

After Cornplanter and Gro-we-na made camp
that evening, they ate their supper of dried venison
and soup and settled down beneath the trees to
sleep. Tomorrow they would arrive at the fort.

"Gro-we-na?" asked her brother. "I have
watched you these last few days. You are quiet and
sad. Was it only to keep your mother from worry?"

Gro-we-na could not answer. Her feelings were
too confused. Cornplanter, the Old Queen, Hai-wa
and his family, and her many friends had been so
wonderful to her. They were her family now. She
had been happy with them for years. She had no
desire to leave them. But now memories filled her
mind, and she felt a calling to the people in them.
They were her family, too. Her blood. She was no

longer sure what she would do when she saw these people — the ones who called her Nellie.

"Gro-we-na, you worry your brother. I bring you to these people only so there will be an end of this in your life — so they will not bother with you anymore. I must be able to trust you."

Gro-we-na's heart beat hard as she looked into his eyes. "Brother, I will not leave you without your permission. I promise to never leave you unless you let me go."

The next morning Gro-we-na dressed in her best clothes, and the two started out before the sun was awake. The river they followed served as their trail. It was very noisy and roared like a hungry panther.

Cornplanter told her stories of the Great Falls and how there was no sound louder than the water spirits beating their wings over the rocky cliffs of the falls. At Fort Niagara, though a long walk from the falls, she would still hear the great beating wings.

Gro-we-na listened as they rode, but she could not think about his words. She was afraid. Old feelings that had been tucked deep inside her began to surface. She remembered her fear when she and Robert were stolen from their cabin. She remembered the long hard march, her bruised feet, and her fatigue. It had been longer than three harvests now, but the memories returned.

Just when it seemed that these memories of fear and hardship would take over, Gro-we-na thought about Cornplanter's kindness to her. In her mind she saw the smile of the Old Queen who cared for her so well. She heard Hai-wa's constant chatter and remembered his gift of the little gray mouse.

What would she do? How could she leave the people who loved her? How could she walk away from the promise of her own fire and a fine husband? Surely the old life would no longer fit her, just as the little skirt no longer fit her.

As they neared the fort Gro-we-na and Cornplanter passed many warriors and chiefs along the trail who called out greetings. Each time they were greeted they stopped, and Cornplanter introduced his sister to the young men of the many camps. It was Gro-we-na's time for joy, a time to survey her future with a young man of her dreams. But for Gro-we-na there was no joy, and Cornplanter seemed to sense it.

Soon the trail by the river opened to a crossing place. Fort Niagara with its great stone walls stood facing them on the other side of the river. Here Colonel Johnson and others would address the chiefs and warriors.

Hoping to catch a glimpse of Cornplanter and their daughter Nellie, the Lytle family waited across the river. Others waited with them. The officers and their wives wanted to witness this bittersweet meeting and to aid Mrs. Lytle when the time came for her daughter to leave her arms.

Colonel Johnson instructed the family once again. Cornplanter would not consider giving up the girl nor did he want them to attempt to ransom her. This was only a visit to show them the girl was treated well and to put their hearts at ease.

The Lytle family had not given up hope that Cornplanter would change his mind. There had to be a place in his heart where he could understand what they had suffered and allow their daughter to return. But if she did not remember, if they could not have her back, how would they be sure that their daughter was really happy?

As the Lytles watched, the small band of Allegheny Seneca emerged on the opposite shore, the American side. A ferry came for them, since recent heavy rains made it impossible to cross on horseback.

Cornplanter watched his sister with sadness as her eyes searched the opposite shore. He knew that she remembered. His heart was heavy.

For a moment Cornplanter was angry with himself. He should not have brought her here. He should not have stirred the fire of her memories. Now they would live forever in her heart. She would not be able to forgive him. He would not be able to restore the happiness they had enjoyed as a family. His anger turned to confusion. What should he do?

As the boat approached them, Cornplanter's friends held his horses. "Cornplanter, carry the horses across first so we do not have to care for them while you are away with these people."

Cornplanter knew that he would not be gone long. "Stand here with them and wait until I return."

Taking Gro-we-na's hand Cornplanter helped her onto the flat-bottomed boat. Her fingers were icy to the touch, and her face was pale with fear. My sister is in pain, he thought, as an iron chain pulled the boat across the swift-moving water.

As the boat drew near the river bank, Gro-we-na could see the people who stood waiting for her. Suddenly she recognized a face, and the pain she had left in the past expressed itself in one pleading cry. "Mother!"

Gro-we-na jumped from the edge of the boat onto the grassy bank of the river and fell into her mother's arms.

"Nellie, Nellie, my beautiful Nellie," cried her mother over and over again as they held on to one another. Her father stepped forward to wrap his arms around his daughter and the three children completed the circle.

Cornplanter stood watching from the ferry, his heart breaking. But his anger and confusion were gone. His heart had spoken to him. He knew now what he had to do.

Solemnly Cornplanter ordered the man running the ferry to return him to the opposite shore. Seeing Cornplanter's retreat, Colonel Johnson rushed to the river. "What trick is this, Cornplanter?"

Cornplanter was silent. Then he cleared his throat and spoke as if each word came with pain.

"She is theirs. The mother must have her child again. I will return alone."

Cornplanter turned and faced his friends on the opposite shore. He must not show emotion. He was a warrior, a chief. The others would expect him to remain strong.

Nellie watched in shock as the boat returned to the opposite shore where Cornplanter disembarked and mounted his horse. As he turned back to look at the family once again, Nellie lifted her hand in thanks to her brother — Cornplanter, the Seneca chief.

Chapter 10
The Legacy

Juliette and Eleanor sat spellbound as their grand-mother finished the story.

Finally Juliette broke the silence. "Did Nellie miss her Indian family?"

"Well, yes, but she was happy to be free to live a life of her own choosing."

"Did the Lytles go back to Pennsylvania?" asked Eleanor.

"No. Mr. Lytle was afraid that Cornplanter would change his mind and come back for Nellie, so he moved the family across Lake Erie to Detroit. There Nellie met and married a British army offi-cer. They had a baby daughter, but the officer was soon killed in an accident. Nellie eventually met and married John Kinzie, a fur trader."

"That's Grandpa's name!" Juliette shouted.

"Yes, your grandfather was named after his father. It was the first John Kinzie that moved our family to Chicago. He and Nellie carried your grandfather in a cradleboard across the wilderness of the Michigan Territory to a fur trading post near Fort Dearborn."

"You mean Nellie in the story is really Grandpa's mother?" asked Juliette as if she were just beginning to understand that Little Ship Under Full Sail was a real person in her own family.

"Of course, she was my mother," affirmed John Harrison Kinzie who had come into the room near the story's end.

"Did she tell you the story herself?" questioned Eleanor as if she too doubted that someone in her family could have had such an adventure.

"Oh, many times," their grandfather assured them. "But it is your grandmother here who has learned all the stories by heart and even written them in a book."

This time Juliette and Eleanor's attention turned to their grandmother who nodded and smiled.

"I wanted those stories to be a family legacy for years and years to come."

"What's a legacy, Grandma?" Juliette asked.

"A legacy is something handed down from the past. And now I think it's bedtime for you two."

After they were tucked into one of their grandparent's big feather beds and left to fall asleep,

Juliette thought about her family and all their adventures. She nudged Eleanor. "Are you asleep?"

"I would be asleep if you hadn't poked me," Eleanor complained.

"You know what I think our legacy is?"

"Grandma already told us what our legacy is. It's the story."

"I think it's our names, too."

"Well, I'm named after the real Nellie," boasted Eleanor.

"But I'm Indian Nellie," Juliette countered, "Little Ship Under Full Sail." She smiled and closed her eyes, enjoying the warmth and comfort of the big feather tick.

Epilogue
The Real Characters

Eleanor "Nellie" Lytle

With her second husband, John Kinzie, Nellie moved to a trading post on the St. Joseph River in what is now southwestern Michigan with her daughter and baby son, John Harrison Kinzie. Nellie's experiences with the Seneca helped the family make friends with Chief To-pe-ne-bee and his Potawatomi people.

When John Kinzie heard of a chance to buy a trading post in the tiny settlement at Chicago, he and Nellie moved again. John built the family a house on the north bank of the Chicago River facing the new Fort Dearborn. As time went by he also opened trading posts in what is now Illinois and southern Wisconsin. The family, however, continued to live in Chicago.

Nellie and John Kinzie raised a family of five children. During the War of 1812 Nellie and her family escaped death by listening to the warnings of Indian messengers. They urged the Kinzies to leave their home because the British and their Indian allies planned an attack. John Kinzie

immediately sent Nellie and the children back to
the safety of Chief To-pe-ne-bee's village. The officer in charge at Fort Dearborn, however, waited to
leave. When he did order an evacuation, many of
his men and their families were attacked and
killed in what is called the Fort Dearborn
Massacre. In 1816 the Kinzie family returned to
Chicago and rebuilt their lives in a more peaceful
time.

Juliette and John Harrison Kinzie

Nellie and John's oldest son, John Harrison Kinzie,
went to work for the American Fur Company on
Mackinac Island. There he met and traveled with
Lewis Cass, Governor of the Michigan Territory.
John was noted for being able to speak several
Indian languages.

While on business in Boston in 1827, young
John Kinzie met and married Juliette Magill.
John's family intrigued Juliette. She listened to the
wonderful stories of the Kinzie family, including
Nellie's life as a Seneca. Later in her life she pub-
lished these stories in a book called *Wau-Bun, The
Early Days in the North-West*.

Juliette and John were not without their own
tales of adventure. Shortly after John was put in

charge of the Indian Agency in Chicago, the Black Hawk War broke out in Illinois. Fearing for the safety of her family, Juliette slept with two pistols under her pillow during that time.

In honor of Gro-we-na, Juliette and John Kinzie named their second child Eleanor Lytle Kinzie. They considered her the family's most willful child, always the ring leader of any trouble. They also called her Little Ship Under Full Sail whenever she demonstrated the headstrong wilfulness that was so evident in her grandmother. This trait, they believed, had come from Gro-we-na's life with the Indians.

William and Eleanor Kinzie Gordon

Although they lived on the frontier, John and Juliette Kinzie insisted that their children be well educated. When Eleanor reached the age of eighteen they sent her to a girls school in New York City. Through a friendship with Eliza Gordon she met and married William Washington Gordon II, a student at Yale. The couple lived in Savannah, Georgia, and eventually had six children, including Juliette Magill Kinzie Gordon who was also nicknamed Little Ship Under Full Sail.

Juliette Gordon

Juliette Gordon grew up to be Juliette Gordon Low, founder of the Girl Scouts. In the spirit of her strong, independent great-grandmother for whom she was named, Juliette had the drive and determination to establish Girl Scout troops around the country. She taught girls what she had learned in part from the stories of her great-grandmother's life — self-reliance, domestic and outdoor skills, physical endurance, a love and respect of nature, and a responsibility to care for your family and those around you. These were lessons that enabled the first Little Ship Under Full Sail to survive and thrive in a sea of events and conflict that might easily have ended her life.

Cornplanter, or Ki-on-twog-ky

There has never been anything recorded concerning Cornplanter's anguish over the loss of Gro-we-na or how he explained the affair to the Old Queen. It is known that he lived a long life, dying in 1836.

A war chief, Cornplanter had been hesitant about fighting during the American Revolution. He felt the Iroquois should stay out of the white man's war. "War is war," he told other Iroquois. "Death is

death. A fight is a hard business." He finally gave
in to pressure and several times helped the British.

In 1784, a year after his sister's release,
Cornplanter negotiated with Americans on behalf
of the Senecas and their land. He also met with
Presidents George Washington and Thomas
Jefferson concerning the rights of the Seneca
people.

During the War of 1812 Cornplanter supported
the American cause, convincing his people to do so
as well. He allowed Quakers into his village to help
the Senecas learn new skills when they could no
longer rely on hunting or the fur trade as a way of
life. He also encouraged men to join the women
working in the fields to help increase their farming
economy.

Later in his life, Cornplanter turned against
contact with whites at the urging of Handsome
Lake, a half-brother who became a Seneca prophet.
To help fight the drunkenness and despair experienced by many Indians, Handsome Lake preached
that the Iroquois must return to the traditional
Indian way of life and take part in religious cere-
monies. Cornplanter is said to have destroyed all of
the gifts given to him by military officials and to

have helped spread Handsome Lake's message.

Cornplanter died in Warren County, Pennsylvania, in 1836. In 1950 the Army Corps of Engineers built the Kinzua Dam on the lands of the Senecas, flooding over ten thousand acres. Today the site of Cornplanter's village and grave lies beneath the waters of the reservoir.